ROSE CHASE

Copyright

Book Cover by GetCovers

Also by

Volkov Bratva:
The Bratva's Bride
The Bratva's Beast
The Bratva's Bounty (11/2024)
The Bratva's Belle (2025)
The Bratva's Beloved (2025)

East Coast Syndicate:
Cardinal (8/24)

Serial Lover:
Killer in the Sheets
Guilty of Love (TBA)

Umbra Demon:
Under My Bed

Content Warning

This book is a darkish paranormal romance that contains content that some may find triggering or disturbing. Contents include: explicit language, explicit violence, sexual violence, abuse, alcohol and drug use, explicit sexual scenes, dub-con/CNC, BDSM elements and tones, mentions of assault, primal play, edge play (breath play, restraints), anal, knotting.
Listen, MMC is a shadow demon so there is going to be some shadow play.

If such content triggers you then please do not continue any further or be mindful of skipping areas of trigger!

Dedication

These shadow princes live in my head rent-free, so I'm gonna make them live in yours rent-free, too! Get ready to tie the knot with this wolfish demon.

In My Closet

Umbra Demon Book 2

Rose Chase

Blurb

"I GOT A GOLDEN retriever... Demon."

Did I expect to get another pet when I moved into my first, and probably only, ever house? No, no, I did not. Especially since this pet came with claws, sharp teeth, and horns. Oh, and not to mention, he did not come from this realm.

I only hoped for a quiet little home to write my life away in my stories, but apparently, that is too much to ask for.

Valphan isn't too bad, though, after I look past the fact that he creeps on me from the closet in my room—yeah, totally not weird. Well, and the fact he is a jealous little turd who chases everyone and everything away from me, but that's to protect me from all the bad in the world.

Honestly, though, he is delightful and protective for a demon.

Never does a night go by that I am lonely because he is always there to blanket me in his shadowy embrace, and I can always sleep soundly at night knowing he is watching over me constantly—seriously, does he even sleep!?

It is impossible to resist his acceptance and adoration of me with time. Especially during the nights with me on his lap on the couch, where he lets me pick his brain for story ideas.

Then, when he goes to the ends of the world for me, I knew I became damned with him until the end of eternity.

Contents

Pronounciations 1

1. Gracie 2
2. Valphan 6
3. Gracie 10
4. Valphan 16
5. Gracie 26
6. Valphan 32
7. Gracie 39
8. Valphan 47
9. Gracie 53
10. Valphan 61
11. Gracie 69

12. Valphan 83
13. Gracie 87
14. Valphan 94
15. Gracie 102
16. Valphan 112
17. Gracie 121
18. Valphan 130
19. Epilogue: Gracie 136
20. Epilogue: Valphan 148
Thank you! 155
About the Author 157

Pronounciations

- **Aesophedus:** Ee-soft-fee-dus
- **Amaldin:** Ah-maul-don
- **Kastoron:** Kas-tore-on
- **Levianth:** Leh-vi-anth
- **Tezrias:** Tez-re-as
- **Valphan:** Val-fawn
- **Zaesiel:** Zay-see-ale

Chapter 1

Gracie

"HOLY SHIT."

I couldn't tell if the rattling sound was my bones shaking from excitement or the piece of paper in my trembling hands.

"Shit can't be holy," my friend Stella chuckled, mocking her demon boyfriend.

That was still so weird to say and think about: a demon boyfriend. Lover? Partner? Actually, anything with the word demon in front of it should not be normal by any means. What made it all the weirder was the fact it would eventually become the norm between my friend and me because her demonic lover wasn't going anywhere.

The fact that my friend was a demon's soulmate was bizarre to me. Out of all the creatures that were intensely loyal and loving, a demon was the last thing to come to my mind, but hey, what did I know? I was just another "annoying and brainless human," to quote Kastoron, Stella's demon soulmate.

"Your parents are going to have an aneurysm when they find out their precious daughter will be moving out," Stella commented with a dry chuckle. But it's about time you get away from them. Seriously, I don't know how you've put up with them for the past year."

"Girl, you and me both. I'm surprised I'm not bald from pulling at my hair so much." It was definitely thinner with way too many split ends after the year, though.

A heavy exhale deflated from my chest as I bundled my long baby pink hair up and brought it in front of my face, frowning at the sad sight of my lifeless strands.

"I'm Surprised they didn't dye your hair back to your natural color or shave you while you were asleep," Stella remarked with a surprised but satisfied smile and nod.

"Only because I was smart enough to put a surface bolt on the door when I had to move my ass back to their place." It probably helped that I lived in their shed, too, because that meant I wasn't physically connected to their house, thus limiting their access to me.

My parents were real pieces of work; that was a given. If I had any other option at the time, I wouldn't have moved back to my parent's place after the whole apartment complex I resided in was burned down by some stupid arson attack. If Stella had her a place back then, I would have moved in with her, but she still lived in a tiny studio apartment.

No matter. I didn't care about any of that anymore. The past is the past, and nothing can be done about it now. I couldn't care less about my parents, either, after my cousin gave me my inheritance letter from my grandma, who had been dead for five years.

I was low-key pissed at the fact I could have had my place five years ago. There weren't any stipulations to my inheritance from what my cousin told me and what I confirmed in Grandma's will and inheritance letter. It just literally never made it into my hands. I was twenty-two years old five years ago, so any clause to wait until I was "of age" wouldn't be valid because I was over eighteen. It boggled both me and my cousin, but we decided to leave it because there was no point in pondering it.

"Are you sure it's wise to go there tonight? I mean, you haven't even seen the place yet, and honestly, if it's been sitting there for five years untouched... Is it even livable still?" Stella's lips twisted with concern as she helped me load the last of my stuff into the trunk of my car.

"My cousin took a look the other day and got everything reconnected and turned back on. The place still runs smoothly and is mostly furnished, too." I beamed with a grin and giddy squeal. "Man, my own place, for free!"

Yeah, good luck getting a damn apartment in this shitty Oregon economy, let alone a whole fucking house. I didn't give a shit if the house was from the late 1900s; a functioning house at no cost to me was a godsend!

"I would change the locks as soon as possible and maybe get a damn security system in place to keep your parents out. You know how much they're gonna blow when they come home later and find you and all your stuff gone without a word," Stella suggested with a concerned smile. "I think I still have some spare locks from when I changed mine if you want them," she offered.

"I'll swing by your place tomorrow to grab them. Honestly, anything to save me money, I'll take." Yeah, call me a cheap-ass Asian; I had no shame about accepting free shit from anyone. Hell, if I passed something labeled free on the streets, I took it.

Rolling her eyes, Stella pulled me into a quick hug. "Be careful. Text me when you get there," she murmured against my shoulder before pulling away. "I'll try to swing by the day after to help you unpack and settle."

Rejecting her with a confident smile and a shake of my head, I waved a small hand in the air."Spend time with your demon, babe. Pretty sure he's gonna go through Stella withdrawals if you don't spend some time with him soon," I joked with a soft chuckle.

Scoffing a soft laugh, I lightly shoved at her shoulder playfully. "Also, please don't teach him how to use technology anymore. Do you have any idea how much he was blowing up your phone throughout the whole day yesterday while we were out at that wedding?"

He was rather needy for a rough, tough demon, which made him rather cute.

Laughing softly in response, she shook her head at me before bidding me farewell and leaving in her vehicle.

"Whelp." Taking a deep breath, I patted the trunk of my car with an excited smile before whistling for my dog. "Goldie! Let's go, buddy!"

The golden retriever mix instantly shot up from his spot on my parents' porch at the call of his name, bolting right to me and lying at my feet with his wagging tail.

"Let's go home."

Chapter 2

Valphan

HOME.

No.

This warmth was too blissful to be home.

A sweet voice, like the screams of the tormented, pulled me from my slumbering grave.

My whole body became enveloped in a strange embrace as I fully woke. I opened my heavy eyelids to a poorly lit room, dimly illuminated by the moonlight streaming through an open window beyond an open door.

Shit, how long have I been asleep? Where am I even?

It felt like an eternity since I closed my eyes and fell into a never-ending darkness. There were many times when I questioned if my slumber had been death, but I always went back on the idea because death meant nonexistence. I wouldn't or shouldn't be aware of anything if I were truly dead.

What even happened?

I hated the empty feeling in my head, even though I knew my thoughts were there. They were all muddled in a thick fog.

Groaning lowly, I slowly stood, hissing and cursing when I hit my head on some shelf. After a few slow blinks, my vision returned to full focus, and I adjusted to the dark area around me.

Both sides of me were lined with rows of wooden shelves, with a rod stretching down the room's length, which seemed quite long. Backing up to the room's entrance, I carefully soaked in every inch of it. The 10 x 13-foot room seemed to be a closet or storage room, which was odd because it seemed rather excessive for a closet or storage room.

Also, I don't remember houses having such spaces. Then again, I don't remember houses having such nice wooden floors, decorated walls, embroidered curtains, or... What the heck was that contraption on that desk, even?

Suddenly, bright lights flashed out of nowhere, causing me to let out a growling hiss at the harsh assault on my poor eyes.

Rotten balls of Lucifer!

The wooden floorboards creaked under my weight as I stumbled backward deeper into the closet's darkness, shielding my eyes with my arms.

What in the frozen pits of home is that light? Am I under some kind of attack?

A snarling growl from the main room made me peer over my arms to see the source of the noise. Expecting some rabid beast, I was sorely confused and disappointed at the mutt I saw hunched at the doorway with its teeth bared in my direction.

"Goldie, quit it. That's just an empty closet." I immediately focused on finding the source of that melodic voice, the one that woke me from my madness in darkness.

More importantly, I wanted to seek the voice to put a face to the enchantress who set fire to my soul.

Sweet Lilith.

The female human took no notice of me as I slowly approached the doorway, being mindful to keep myself hidden in the shadows. She was strange-looking and wore clothes that weren't typical of what I knew females wear. I have seen demonesses dressed in such ways, but the humans I knew wouldn't dare show as much as an ankle. Yet this woman wore a dress that came to above her knees, and half of her chest hung out because of the dress's plunging neckline. I wasn't complaining about the nice sight of such beauty. If this was how the human males allowed their females to dress now, then I fully supported it.

"Goldie, what is your problem? Do you see a mouse or something?" Her voice sounded like a choir of tortured souls to my ears.

So lovely.

Even when she scolded the mutt, she sounded nice while irritated.

However, one thing I couldn't ignore was her hair. Why in Lucifer's name was it such a shade of pink? Had the humans fully mastered magic to change their appearance? It looked odd, and usually, I hated such soft and bright colors, but I wasn't too bothered by hers. The only thing that bothered me was the urge to run my fingers through those long locks to determine if they were as soft as they looked.

Unfortunately, that urge would need to be settled some other time. Much to my displeasure, the woman turned and left the room before I could make it out of the room I was in. I couldn't go after her either because when I tried to cross the room's threshold, a force slammed into me, preventing me from going beyond the door frame.

What in Lucifer's balls?

Irritated, I held my hand up against this invisible wall, pressing against it to test its strength. The irritation quickly turned into full-blown anger the moment I realized my situation.

"Fuck!" I angrily shouted, pounding against the magical barrier.

Chapter 3

Gracie

~1 month later~

RUBBING THE BACK OF my neck, I looked around the closet warily while wrapping a protective arm around my body.

Something didn't feel right. Well, let me correct myself: something still doesn't feel right.

I don't know what it was, but I had constantly felt on edge for the past two weeks, especially in my room. The feeling of bugs crawling under my skin was akin to how I felt at Stella's house, knowing Kastoron was around and watching me from every shadow in the damn place, which was very odd because my home was definitely not haunted! I made sure of it by bringing in a priest and a demonologist, both of whom checked the house out as perfectly safe and clear of otherworldly entities.

So, why did I feel such unease in my own home?

A chill ran down my spine for the umpteenth time today from the feeling of something brushing over me as if someone blew air onto me. If this sensation hadn't happened so often, I would have chalked it up to the AC or heat kicking on, but I didn't hear the telltale creak of the systems running most of the time. Then, I felt my spine straighten and shake.

This uneasiness could have stemmed from the fact I was in a new place, but I've been in new places before, lived on my own, and whatnot, so this shouldn't be anything foreign to me. The area I lived in wasn't bad either. It wasn't the shady part of town or anything. Actually, it was a quaint place located in a very family-friendly neighborhood, the one where everyone knew each other and was friends with each other. So, it couldn't be the environment... Right?

Shuddering loudly, I quickly reached out to steady myself using one of the shelves when my knees went weak and buckled under me.

What the fuck?

It felt like something slithered its way up my legs and stroked my inner thighs. God, I felt violated, and the worst part was that the feeling lingered as if someone had settled their hands on my thighs.

Well, if I didn't feel violated before, I definitely did when the touch moved up and pressed right along my covered cunt. Whimpering, I let my knees give out completely, letting my body slump to the ground in a panting heap as the heat of arousal filled my body.

What the hell is going on? Why am I so turned on? What's happening?

A pounding noise filled my ears the longer I remained inside the closet, and it took me a while to realize it was my own heart ramming against my ribcage from the adrenaline surging through my body. My body was telling me to get the fuck out of here and scramble out the door that was a few feet from me. Yet, I couldn't bring myself to.

As violating as this felt, something about it felt good, fitting almost. I don't know why or how, but whatever was happening grew on me. Yeah, it felt like some weird force was touching me, but I felt safe.

I probably have to get a priest back in here to exorcise the whole damn place after this, but whatever was touching me was being gentle about it. And honestly, it was kind of harmless, like it wasn't penetrating me or shedding my clothes. Then again, could it even do that? Maybe this was the extent of its reach.

Granted, this is all playing on the fact there was something in here with me right now and touching me, and not because I was hallucinating everything. Dear God, I hope I wasn't hallucinating all of this somehow because that would be very concerning. Also, I was trying to dissuade my guilt about the fact I was coming from this whole thing to make myself feel less hysterical.

Sighing softly with pleasure, I widened my legs slightly to give the ghostly touch more access to my covered sex. This was so lewd, but I didn't care. I was so close and needed to come so badly. And whatever this thing was, it knew how to get me there. The moment I gave it more access, I could feel more pressure against my aching clit.

"Fuck." I gasped deeply, letting my mouth hang open slightly in a silent moan as I felt the familiar crash of my orgasm shake my body.

Strangely, as I did this, something warm washed over my face, particularly my lips. Was whatever this was kissing me? I swear, it felt like being devoured by a mouth while mine was stuffed with a warm tongue. But it couldn't be, right? Because this thing wasn't real.

Once my orgasm passed with the feeling of arousal, my sense of rationality came back in full force. Needless to say, I scrambled out of there faster than a rabbit bolting from a predator.

Strangely enough, I felt normal when I cleared out of the closet. Sure, I had that sensation of eyes on me, like a peeping Tom through the windows, but I didn't feel my personal space become crowded like inside the closet.

Speaking about the closet, I had to do something about that.

Getting up to my feet, I shuffled over to my desk to snatch my phone up and call Stella. I mean, I couldn't think of anyone else better to deal with paranormal shit than a demon.

"Hey, what's up?" The wave of relief at Stella's voice caused me to sigh.

Bypassing a friendly greeting, I let my frantic words fly out of my mouth as I hopped into bed. "Stella, I need you to get your ass over here with Kas and figure out what the fuck is going on with my house."

"Whoa, whoa, hold up. What's going on? Like, start from the beginning, girl, because I thought you had your damn house cleared by a shit ton of people already. So, why do you need me and Kassie—oh shut up and let me talk on the phone, you jerk—sorry, Kassie was throwing a fit about his name again. But, sorry, explain." I could hear some faint destruction from Stella's end in the background, probably Kastoron—her demon soulmate—throwing a fit with the plastic houseware.

Sighing heavily, I let my wary eyes dart over to my closet, staring holes into it as if I could conjure up the figment of my imagination. "It's stupid, but ever since I moved in, every time I go into my closet, I just feel strange, and it always feels like someone or something is constantly watching me whenever I'm in my room." Talking about it now, it was really weird because it only happened when I was in my room.

"Okay, try to explain strange because that's a little vague. Like, are you sure you're not a little too paranoid from Kassie? I'm not trying to sound dismissive, but he can trip people up pretty good." Well, I didn't blame her for asking and possibly thinking that because, to be honest, her demon mate still scared the shit out of me more often than not.

"Okay, strange as in I feel like someone is physically there, crowding my personal bubble, and touching me. Honestly, it almost feels exactly like Kas's shadows when he fucks around with me when I visit. And then, just now, whatever it was, made me come." I don't know why I chose to blurt out that last part, but it manifested into the world before my mind could rein it in.

Cue the awkward silence because, yep. "Wait. What?" Yeah, you and me both, sister, because that was my reaction to it all right now. "Hold up. Okay, what? Like, did you actually see something touch you or...?"

"No, that's the thing! I never see anything, just feel it. It's like those people on the paranormal show that are like sensitives, or whatever, where they can feel the presence of spirits and shit, I think. I guess. I don't know." Frustrated and defeated, I let out a whimpering sigh as I crumpled up in bed, pulling my blanket over me. "And, like, Goldie's been acting strange since we moved here. He's fine everywhere in the house except my room. The moment we go in, he goes into protective mode and is not happy about the closet one bit."

Okay, my dog's reaction probably should have been a flag for me to dig into the issue further because it was really out of character for him. Initially, I thought it was some critter who'd gotten into the house, but come on, two straight weeks of my sweet dog reacting like so towards the damn closet should have slapped me in the face.

"Just... Please? Can you and Kas please come over tomorrow and see if everything is okay or if I'm just going crazy?" I could very well be letting my imagination get the best of me after going through so many edits of so many stories.

"Hey, yeah, just don't sleep in your room tonight. We'll come over first thing tomorrow morning to check things out," Stella said in a calm voice.

"Excuse you? We? I don't—ow!" A small commotion ensued from Stella's side following Kastoron's voice.

A moment later, Stella's voice came back online. "We'll be there at 10 AM tomorrow. Just be safe for tonight, alright? And if you need to, come over and spend the night at my place. We can return in the morning after a night's rest." Stella offered kindly.

Sighing softly, I shook my head with a chuckle. "It's okay, I'll just sleep on the couch—"

SLAM!

Or not...

Chapter 4

Valphan

I THINK THE FUCK not.

How dare she decide to deprive me of her lovely presence after I gave her such a wonderful orgasm? Did our moment mean nothing to her? She let me touch her, caress her body until it trembled against me, and then she let me kiss her and claim her mouth with my tongue.

I mean, yeah, she did run away like a scared rabbit, but that's because she wasn't thinking straight from her high crashing. Well, and maybe not being able to see me freaked her out a little, but I couldn't help that I was trapped in some limbo state because of whatever fuck up happened with the gate.

"Stella! I can't get out!" And she wouldn't, not unless I let her. My pretty little mate could pull on the door all she wanted, but it wouldn't budge unless I released my shadow lock from it. "As in, it won't open! And no, it's not locked! It just slammed shut and is like jammed shut or something!"

I felt a little bad for inciting fear in my mate, but I had no other choice. She couldn't hear my voice, so telling her not to go was pointless as it was the equivalent of shouting into a void. I couldn't physically go out there to stop her either because, again, I was trapped inside this stupid closet. The only thing that could go a little way beyond the barrier was my shadows, but even that had its limits.

"Please, hurry!" She sobbed into her handheld device, a 'phone' as I've heard her call it.

Honestly, humans have evolved so strangely over the years. Granted, centuries have passed, so I would be surprised if they didn't evolve. Still, it was quite a shock to me to see all these new gadgets they have. At least it was nice to see that they had efficient plumbing, running water, fresh and clean water, and electricity. Living on Earth back then was worse than living back home. At least we had those things back home through the use of magical relays, receptors, and runes.

Unfortunately, humans weren't blessed with magical abilities or the abilities to harness the free-flowing magic in the air unless they were gifted, and very few were gifted. However, after seeing my share of horrors from humans, I could understand why God chose to make humans different from us higher beings in that sense.

Many of them were already crazy as they were without magical capabilities. Seriously, they already did so much damage to themselves and their society with their own ambitions and absurd beliefs. I never thought I'd see more death here on earth than back home.

Humans were really a different breed. They were kind of stupid. Seriously, so much mindless murder and such backward ass logic.

Things seemed different now regarding independence for the females of the population—thank the high Heavens and low levels of Hell. It was disheartening to see women being oppressed by men when I had agreed to come to Earth with Aesophedus and the other shadow princes to watch over and help humanity. Also, we were in charge of regulating supernatural entities that humans couldn't touch to keep them from making trouble with God's little paradise away from Heaven.

So, it was refreshing to see my little mate free to her own devices without anyone around to control her. It would have been a bloody mess if she had some stupid human male bullying her around. Yeah, sometimes males were sweet and good to their partners, but for the most part, from what I observed during my time conscious and aware, they weren't.

If I had it my way, half the population back then would have been freezing to death in my home layer of Hell. If they couldn't appreciate the warmth of love from a female, then they shall have no warmth at all.

Too bad I wasn't allowed to drag them down myself.

My only job on earth was to guide spirits through the gate or go after them and drag them through it if they weren't willing. Besides being the gatekeeper, I was a protector, not an aggressor or hunter like some of the others.

"Hey! Let me out! I don't know who you are or what you are, but you better let me out!" My mate screamed into the air while whipping her head around.

I knew she couldn't hear me, but speaking aloud kept me sane. "Or else what? What are you going to do, my little blessing?" I chuckled out loud to myself as I leaned against the frame of the closet, crossing my arms and watching her pace angrily around her room.

If only I could grab her into my arms right now and snuggle her like there was no tomorrow. I wanted to tackle her onto that bed, trap her in my arms, press that plush body of hers against mine, squish that face of hers in my large hand, and spoil her with kisses. I would kill for a minute to snuggle with her right now.

I fucking loved how much she's filled out over the past weeks. It was subtle, but it was progress. My little mate wasn't too happy about having to buy new pants because she went up a size recently, but I was more than happy with how her ass and thighs were filling out. Top-wise, she had a defined waist but a small chest and narrow shoulders, and it definitely wasn't as filled out as her bottom half. Not that it mattered to me because she was as cute and snuggly as one of those stupid stuffed bears of hers.

Defeated, my Gracie let out a groan as she threw her hands into the air and let them slap against her thighs before she plopped into the chair at her desk. Then, her head snapped to me, or the closet, more likely. "What do you even want with me? Why won't you show yourself?" It was as if she could see me, but that wasn't possible given this stupid curse.

A long sigh dragged out of me as I looked at her with a deep frown, my hand pressing against the invisible barrier. "I would if I could." I wanted to so badly. I wanted to show myself to her, let her see her glorious mate, maybe flex a bit for her because human females tend to love it when males show off.

Letting out another sigh, I rested my head against the barrier and softly banged my fist against it.

Stupid barrier.

And the more damning thing was my inability to figure a way through. I knew what was wrong but couldn't fix it because the gate was beyond my reach. I needed to examine the gate fully to see what parts were messed with to cause this barrier and my prison.

The squeak and creak of her chair and the sounds of scraping against wood turned my full attention back to my mate. Her luscious hips swayed with each step she took toward me—okay, the closet, more likely because, again, she couldn't see me.

Much to my disappointment, she stopped right at the threshold, literally a thread away from my grasp. "Listen, I know, whoever or whatever you are, that you are in there." She huffed with a glare into the closet, which right now was right into my midsection. "I don't know what you want with me, but I don't know you or even see you or want anything to do with you. So, please, just let me out. Whoever or whatever you are, my friends can help you in a bit once they get here."

"Doubtful." I mused with a scoffing laugh.

The idiot priest and demonologist (yeah, I had a laugh with that one) didn't find me out. So, I highly doubted her friends would do a better job than these 'officials' she had brought in over the weeks.

Okay, I had my doubts until her friends actually showed up. The moment I felt the familiar presence of a shadow prince, yeah, I was saved and/or fucked, depending on how my little mate weaved things.

"Gracie! Open the door!" A familiar female voice shouted through the pounding of the door.

A deeper, raspier voice 'tsked' on the other side, "She can't. It's locked with magic." Never thought I'd be so happy to hear *his* voice—at least, I think it was *his* voice.

A loud *thud* and *bang* filled the area, and the door was thrown off its hinges. The moment the door was gone, two figures revealed themselves. The female was familiar; she had been here numerous times, being my mate's friend.

The male, though. "Kastoron! Thank Lucifer's balls! Sweet screams of torment! Kastoron!" I knew letting my glee come out verbally was pointless, but I couldn't contain it at the familiar sight.

I could barely keep my eyes on my mate as she ran to her friend's arms because I was too focused on Kastoron stalking warily into the room. I'd deal with the jealousy later. What mattered now was getting out of this damn trap.

"You definitely have something here, that's for sure," Kastoron commented as he stood inches from the closet doorway, studying it carefully.

"Go inside and see if you can find something." My mate shooed Kastoron forward with a few flicks of her hand, making me chuckle out of amusement at the sight of her boldness toward my fellow friend.

Kastoron did not seem too pleased with that, not that I blamed him. Like the little sass he is, he spun around and faced the two females with his hands on his hips. "I think. The. Fuck. Not. You couldn't pay me enough to go into that gateway with no way out." He sneered while jabbing a finger toward the closet.

"What do you mean? I go in and out just fine." My mate retorted with a soft glare at Kastoron.

With a sneer, he pointed a finger at the females. "Because you're a human." Then, he pointed at himself, "I'm a demon, a completely different entity from you and Stella.

If I go through there, I ain't coming back until whatever is wrong with this gate is fixed."

And that's when all my hope went into the void because Kastoron outlived his use. Then again, I didn't expect much from him in the first place. He may be powerful and a grade-A trickster, but he was useless regarding nitty-gritty dimensional magic. I had to give him some credit, though; he did figure out that something was wrong with the gate and that there was a gate present without having to spend much time investigating.

Leaning against the wall next to the closet, he crossed his arms and gave a nonchalant shrug of his shoulders. "Honestly, you could live just fine. Whatever is stuck is stuck. It won't manifest or go beyond the closet. It won't be able to harm you, either. The most you'll feel are those phantom touches, but that's about it."

Then, pensively, he looked into the closet again, even going as far as to reach out towards the closet but stopping right before crossing. "It feels... Familiar... And whatever is behind there doesn't feel malevolent, so you should be relatively safe." Now, I wanted to punch him in the face for insinuating that I could harm my mate.

"Oh, like how you're not bad?" Gracie remarked mockingly.

The spunk of human females in this day and age on earth still somewhat surprises me. If she were a demoness, then I wouldn't bat an eye, but I couldn't help but admire the backbone of my mate.

"Hey, I never... Uhh nevermind... Just... You'll need a different expertise to help you fix and get rid of this gateway. The only ones I can think of besides Aesophedus are Valphan and possibly Levianth. Your best shot will be Valphan since he is literally a gatekeeper, so this is all up in his jam."

Kastoron gestured widely at the closet. "Unfortunately, Valphan is MIA, as in no one, not even Aesophedus, knows where the fuck he is."

It's because I'm right here, you dingbat!

Frustrated, I pounded my fists against the barrier with an angry cry.

"Whoa! Someone's not happy about something I said." Kastoron reacted with a surprised look in my direction. "Well, either way, you should get this fixed sooner than later before other issues start to show up, literally."

"What do you mean other issues?" My mate questioned with narrowed eyes, not sounding too happy with Kastoron.

"Dimensional gateways are usually set up in that they draw in lost spirits and entities. Also, entities are drawn to it because it means they can pull shit from the other side over to this side. So, you're gonna start to have unsavory visitors of the ghostly and demonic kind sooner rather than later." Kastoron paused briefly to study the area around the closet with a furrowed face. "Though... Something about this gate... It should be a hotbed of paranormal activity, yet I don't sense anything besides whatever is in the closet for miles."

Yeah, because I'm here, you horn head!

Another angry pound against the barrier caused Kastoron to flinch slightly. "I don't know if it has to do something with the gate itself because I can't see it or if it has to do with whatever is stuck on the other side." A heavy axe of tension hung in the air, ready to descend with the next words. "Which makes me wonder what is on the other side and why it's trapped."

After a long sigh, Gracie took tentative steps toward the closet, stopping inches before it and looking at it with downturned eyes. "So, what now? Besides move, because I ain't doing that." She didn't sound too happy with that idea either.

Obviously, I wasn't because that meant losing my mate. I didn't want that. I'd surely go mad without her presence to keep me anchored. It already killed me to be unable to touch her. The ghosting whispers from my tendrils only soothed the need to an extent, and ghosting her body when she entered the closet served more like torture. The fact she was there and I could somewhat touch her but not fully, nor could I show myself to her, was just cruel.

"I'll contact Aesophedus and Levianth and see what they can do," Kastoron said with a defeated sigh and shrug of his shoulders. "In the meanwhile, just stay safe and try not to piss off whatever is in there, I guess." Scratching his horn, he twisted his face in thought for a second, "And I guess if things start to show up, then you can stay at our place until you figure out your next course of action."

"Fucking hell, how does this shit happen to me?" Gracie groaned into her hands with a frustrated cry. "I just wanted freedom, and when I get it, I get a haunted closet, great." Her voice was saturated with sarcasm at the last bit.

"Hey, could have ended up with a Kastoron, so it's not *that* bad." Her friend tried to cheer her up with an awkward laugh.

"Yeah! My doll has a point. You could have a demon chucking shit at you and scaring you around every corner." And now I wanted to throttle the idiot out the window. I would wonder if he was serious or not, but knowing him... Yeah... I pity the poor human girl who put up with his shit.

"Do you want us to spend the night just in case?" Her friend offered with a concerned frown.

Sheepishly, my mate nodded her head. "Please? It'd make me feel safer."

Well, I didn't like that. I mean, did she not trust me? Did she really think I'd harm her?

Okay, that might have been a little irrational of me because she couldn't have known any of that. Still, it pissed me off.

I would never harm my little blessing.

Chapter 5

Gracie

WELL, WHEN MY DOOR rang, the last person I expected to open it to was an even shorter girl than me.

"Hi there, I'm Emma." She introduced herself with a smile that put the sun to shame as she waved at me.

"Umm hi? I'm sorry for seeming rude, but... Uhh, are you here because of Kastoron? Or are you one of my neighbors, who I'm unaware of, coming by to say hi?" She could very well be one of my neighbors.

I wasn't the most social person around, so I definitely didn't go around introducing myself to everyone after I finished moving, nor did I want to. Yeah, call me a little loner hermit, but that's how I preferred things. It was also because I didn't know how to talk to people properly in person. Online? No problem, mainly because I had a screen to hide behind.

"Well, yes, and no? I'm a detective for the Portland Police, but I'm also a paranormal detective. I don't personally know Kastoron, but my husband does, and that's who Kastoron reached out to." Emma's response somewhat confused me, but I forced myself to swallow the information either way as I stepped aside to let her in.

"And your husband is?" I prodded for an answer as I gestured her over to the couches.

Now, like any normal person, I was expecting an answer and maybe some pictures. Ya know, normal shit.

Not her shadow coming to life!

Yeah, I probably should be somewhat used to seeing shadows have a mind of their own with Kastoron, but I had the foreknowledge of him being around. This literally happened out of nowhere!

Emma's shadow literally popped up off the ground and solidified into a demon with huge bat-like wings, horns on his head, and clawed hands. And here I thought Kastoron looked a little terrifying.

"That would be me." The demon spoke as his figure became more physical. "Levianth, the guardian and hunter, a pleasure to meet you." And his voice was deeper and raspier than Kastoron's, too. "Kastoron told me that you had a gateway to be debugged?"

Okay, this just got a little awkward. "Uhh yeah... It's upstairs in my room. Kastoron's up there with Stella right now."

Great. Not only did I have to put up with one demon, but now I have a second one to put in the mix. Great, just fucking great. What did I do to deserve this!? I've been a good person! I only told white lies when needed and never cheated, stole, or, God forbid, killed. I mean, maybe a fly or spider here and there, but that was the extent of murder by my hands, I swear!

"Listen, I'm sorry... It's just... The whole demon thing is still weird and new to me, and Kastoron didn't inform me exactly who was coming, so I wasn't expecting a sweet-looking girl like you, then the demon popping out of your shadow." I continued to let my awkwardness control my twisting tongue that constantly streamed out every word my mind concocted.

A pair of hands grabbing and jarring me made me shut my mouth. "Gracie, it's okay." Emma chuckled softly while rubbing my shoulders. "We're just here to help, nothing more, nothing less. I mean, I probably should have given you a bit of a heads-up about Levianth. Not many expect my husband to be in my shadow, literally."

Forcing a smile, I averted my eyes and rubbed the back of my neck. "I'm just a little frazzled and weirded out about everything, and I just want to figure out what's going on with my closet."

"We'll do our best, promise," Emma assured me with a bright grin before heading to my room after I took the lead.

The first thing to come out of anyone's mouth the moment Emma and Levianth entered the room was anything but warm. "Kas, you better not have touched anything," Levianth grumbled after nearly shoving Kastoron away from the closet.

"Hey, I know when to not fuck around, this being one of them." Kastoron scoffed with a roll of his eyes. "Not like

I can do much besides tear down the place, which we might have to do because I think the actual doorway is embedded inside the walls or something."

"Whoa, whoa, whoa," I interjected with a frantic wave of my hands, "No one is destroying anything in my place unless it is absolutely necessary. Or if you do, you better put it back together."

Chuckling, Levianth looked at me with a reassuring smile. "Don't worry, nothing is going to be torn apart. There's an easy solution to figuring out the gate and its runes," the bigger demon paused for a second to deadpan at Kastoron, "Without having to kick down some walls."

Levianth settled his hand against the frame of the closet, closed his eyes, and muttered something under his breath. Seconds after he started muttering, the sides of the wall glowed with strange lines of symbols.

"This doesn't look right," Kastoron commented with a deep frown.

Stepping back, Levianth studied everything in a pensive silence before speaking up, "It's not. Someone's tampered with it and removed the keystone."

"Okay, so where does that leave us now?" Not to sound like an ungrateful brat, but I honestly have no idea how all of that played into solving my little problem.

"Well, at least now we know what we need to do to fix the gate, release whatever is trapped in there, then close and destroy the gate," Levianth replied with a flat press of his lips.

"Why can't you just destroy it outright?" Saying it out loud made me wince visibly at how cruel I sounded.

"Because if we don't fix it, then it'll be too unstable to destroy. Yeah, we could try to blow it to bits now, but it could blow back on us badly." I still didn't like the grim tone of

Levianth's voice, and the fact Kastoron had kept his trap shut this whole time didn't ease my nerves anymore.

Crossing my arms, I huffed and jutted a hip out. "What are you two not telling me? There's a huge 'but' in the room, and it's definitely not mine." I snapped with a glare at the two demons.

The two demons looked back and forth at each other for a moment before Levianth's shoulders deflated with his sigh. "We can easily craft a keystone and open the gateway... Fixing it though, that's... Uhh... That's going to be rather tricky since it's not either of our areas of expertise. Aesophedus could figure it out faster than us, but he's pretty caught up with some issue of his own." Dragging his attention around the room, he rubbed the edge of his wings a little. "It's going to take a long stretch of research to properly fix the gate without blowing it up."

Groaning, I ran my hands up my face and into my pink hair, gripping it. "So, I have to put up with whatever the hell you two are releasing in the meantime?" I did not sign up to be a ghost sitter!

"Well, we'll take care of it once it's released. We wouldn't just leave you to deal with something like that." Levianth assured me with a small wave of his hand. "Give me and Kastoron an hour, tops, and we'll have a keystone created and this thing open. You girls go eat a quick snack or something." He dismissed us, shoving us out of the room with some shadow tendrils before shutting the door behind us.

"Rude!" Stella huffed, stomping her foot and groaning frustratedly.

Rude indeed, but we couldn't do anything but wait, unfortunately.

Thankfully, it didn't take a whole hour for the two demons to figure out this keystone business.

Not thankfully, were the results of their efforts.

"Why the fuck is there a demon in my closet!?"

Chapter 6

Valphan

I WORRIED MY INCESSANT pacing would burn a hole through the floor below at the slow rate the two idiots went at with figuring out and crafting a keystone. Granted, I should give them more credit for handling it at the speed they did since it wasn't up their alleyway. Also, I should be grateful for the fact they could free me.

Still, it felt like forever until they fully set the keystone in and opened the gate, letting me out of limbo to their dumbstruck faces.

Seconds passed to minutes as all three of us stood there staring at each other, the two of them looking at me as if they were watching an angel in a gangbang.

My irritation got the best of me in the next second of waiting around for *some* kind of greeting from them, causing me to snark at them. "Oh, Valphan, thank the lowest levels of home that you are fine. Oh, Valphan, you're alive, sweet! Oh Valphan, buddy, there you are." Okay, not the best time to be cracking jokes or whatever, but not even a twitch from any of them.

"Come on, you guys are going to kill me here," I muttered with a roll of my eyes.

Kastoron was the first to make a move toward me after staring at me like an idiot. However, he might as well have been an idiot because of how he reacted.

Scowling, I swatted his hand away when it came toward my face. "Quit!" I snarked. "I might be happy to see you again after all this time, but don't think I won't hesitate to bite your finger off." I playfully threatened Kastoron, who had a huge ass grin on his face.

"Val! Buddy!" Instead of my body, Kastoron was met with a wall of shadows. "Hey, what gives?" He complained after peering around the shadow wall.

"I don't want your stupid to rub off on me." I deadpanned at him before taking a tentative step across the closet entrance, sighing in relief when I didn't feel an unseen wall slam into me.

Unfortunately, my victory was short-lived because I barely made it three small steps before I felt a pull stop me from going further. It felt like there were chains connected to every section of my body to the walls of the closet; literally, it felt like there were metal hooks in my bones.

"Damn, and I thought I had it bad," Kastoron muttered with an apologetic frown at me.

"How long have you been in there, man?" Levianth asked while looking me over with his concerned eyes.

"I don't know." It was the Devil's honest truth. "I only became aware about three weeks ago when my mate moved in, and her soul woke mine up."

"Does everyone just know their soulmate off the bat besides me?" Kastoron grumbled with a string of muttered curses under his breath.

"It's because you're an idiot." Levianth sneered with a mocking laugh.

"Oh shut up, you literally got trapped with your mate, you lucky rat-ass hornhead." Kastoron retorted with a scowl and huff.

Mumbling to himself for a second, he glared holes into Levianth's smirking face for a good minute before softening his expression as he turned his attention to me. "Going based off of when you went missing, I'd say you've been out of it for a little over five centuries."

"Unholy shit." Five centuries?! No. There was no way it's been that long.

Levianth sighed heavily and chuckled softly before pulling out a cellular device from his pocket to show me the brightly lit screen, which made my face fall further.

"Wow, I didn't think it was possible for you to look as white as a ghost, considering how pale you already are." Kastoron snickered at me. "Welcome to the twenty-first century, my friend. Boy, is it going to be a shock for you."

"Better wipe that shell-shocked look off your face before the girls come back up here. Wouldn't want this face to be the first your mate sees of you." Levianth mentioned with a pat on my shoulder as he passed me on his way to open the door.

"Fucking home... Seriously!?" How I hadn't lost my damn mind floating in mindless darkness for so long gripped at my confused mind as I began to pace back and forth inside the closet.

"Girls, come up here!" I heard Levianth shout, a little too happily for my tastes.

Oh, sweet Lucifer, I am not ready for my mate to see me for the first time.

Each soft thump of footfalls on the hardwood floor seemed to mimic my own heart in my chest. Louder and louder everything grew until it all came to a stop the moment I laid my eyes on my beautiful mate.

Whatever worry had sunk its claws into my body, released at the sight of her and the feeling of her presence warming up the room. Well, it all went well until her exclamation.

"Why the fuck is there a demon in my closet!?"

Realistically, her reaction was fair and should have been expected, but the hopeful side of me really wished she had run into my arms and embraced me. Yeah, it was stupid of me to think that'd happen, but one could hope.

"Uhh, so, meet Valphan, The Gatekeeper, shadow prince, a demon from the frozen depths of Hell. Uhh lovely demon, such a sweetheart really, and uhh yeah." Kastoron awkwardly slipped toward the door, grabbing Gracie's friend on the way out. "Have fun getting to know each other!" And he was off with a protestant female in his arms.

Levianth was quick to retreat cowardly with Kastoron. "Well, our job here is done, would love to stick around, but we have cases to work on. Busy, busy, busy." Damn idiot took off faster than Kastoron with his mate being dragged behind him like a ragdoll.

"Ugh! Are you guys serious!?" Stomping over to the door, Gracie stuck her head through to the hallway. "Hey! What am I supposed to do with him!? Hey!"

No response came from the empty house; only Gracie's frustrated grunts and grumbles chimed in the air. Then, the sounds of her soft footsteps filled the air from her pacing.

What happened next took me by surprise.

When she approached me, I thought it was to hug me or get a closer look at me, so I couldn't help but raise a quizzical eyebrow at her when she placed her hand on my bare chest and pushed me into the closet. Only because I let her, though. If I had dug my heels in, even remotely, then she'd be better off moving a built wall.

I planned to let her do what she wanted, but I lunged when she backed away and tried to shut the doors on me. "Whoa, hey." My hands grabbed the edges of the door and forced them back open. "What are you doing, my little blessing?"

Gritting her teeth, she grunted, struggling to push the closet doors shut. "Putting you back in the closet to ignore you and pretend you don't exist so I can go on with my merry life." She strained, her feet squeaking against the wooden floor from her struggle.

Tilting my head, I looked down at her with scrunched-up eyebrows. "Why on earth would you want to do that? Have I wronged you somehow?" Okay, stupid question because I have touched her without her permission on numerous occasions.

"Because I don't want a demon in my life. My life is already weird as it is. I don't need it to be more complicated." She strained through her grunting as she pressed her back against the door to lean her weight against it. "I just want to live a normal life. Is that too hard to ask for?"

"And a normal life constitutes what exactly?" I questioned with a growing smirk as I watched her struggle amusingly.

Letting out an angry cry, she sank to the ground and glared up at me. "I don't know, but it doesn't involve you in it." She huffed, crossing her arms.

"I forget how strange you humans are with your life choices," I muttered aloud, chuckling softly as I squatted down beside her.

Reaching out, I stroked the back of my finger along her soft cheek. Shivers pricked along my back as I relished the feeling of being able to touch her for the first time physically. "You're so soft, like fresh snow." My thoughts slipped out before I knew it, but I didn't care. Seeing the way her cheeks pinkened up was too sweet.

"That is so not a sweet thing to say." The temptation to call her out on her lie hung on the tip of my tongue, but I'd let her have this pass for her sake. "And can you please stop touching me? I'm not a dog." She hissed, smacking my hand away and scrambling away from me with a look of disdain on her face.

It was adorable how she tried to deceive herself and me. Guess humans were still as stubborn as ever.

Slowly, she got back up on her shaky legs and wrapped her arms around herself. "Why are you even still here? You're free, so go." She shooed a hand toward the open door.

I won't lie; her words and actions stung me a little. How could she be so cold toward me? I was her mate, so why? Did she know how much she caused my heart to ache? I might not show it, but I was hurt rather deeply.

"I am still bound to this gate. I can enter the physical realm and remain, but I cannot go beyond a few steps of this... Closet." Bound to a closet, how fucking lovely. I bet Kastoron and Levianth were having a field day with the fact.

"Then fix it, free yourself, and go." Gracie insisted, her hands balling into fists and her feet stomping softly with a deepening frown on her face.

"If only it were that simple, my little blessing." My chest sank with my dry chuckle. "Even if it were, I would not leave you once I was to free myself."

Growling softly, she narrowed her sharp, almond eyes at me. "And why the fuck not?" She looked about ready to slap me with the burning fire in her eyes.

Tilting my head at her with a flat expression, I pondered for a moment if she was truly toying with me. "Why, from the high Heavens to the deepest layers of Hell, would I ever leave my mate?"

"YOUR WHAT!?"

Chapter 7

Gracie

~2 weeks later~

"Stop staring at me!" I snapped at Valphan after whipping my head at him.

Seeing his stupid, smug-ass, lovey-dovey smile turned the heat up under my already boiling pot.

"And rob myself of such a beautiful sight? I think not." He remarked with an amused chuckle, leaning back on his hands. "Besides, what are you going to do about it? Hm?

Make me go back into the closet? Shut the doors? Put up the pathetic screen between us?"

Okay, now I wanted to march over from my desk and slap him across the face for being a smartass. "Go find a different mate! I never agreed to be your mate in the first place, and if that's your only reason for sticking around because of some destined relationship between us, then sorry to break it to you, buddy, but that's not how that shit happens." Yeah, I'd really like to have a conversation with the man in the sky about this issue right about now.

Hey, God, can I get a fucking refund for something I didn't order? Thanks.

Granted, I'd put it in kinder words, but it'd be something along those lines.

Straightening his legs past the closet entryway, he wiggled his clawed feet back and forth. "That's not how it works, little blessing. We were lucky enough to be destined the moment we were created. One does not 'choose' a mate, not like those silly stories of yours about the werewolves and stuff." His voice held no contempt toward me for my spiteful words, making me feel a little bad for snapping at him.

"It will come to you with time. But I won't rely solely on our mate bond to have you fall for me." I hated how confident he sounded with his grind. "As from the messages I have seen from the human males of this day and age, I got the rizz."

Now, I wanted to dig a hole and bury myself alive from the secondhand embarrassment. Unable to face the embarrassment lounging on the floor a few feet from me, I buried my face into my hands and let out a groan. "No, please don't ever say that ever again. Do not try to use any slang you see, just, don't." Boarding up the closet didn't seem like a bad idea now.

"Why? You respond well to those stupid messages on your phone from those men?" And now I've pissed off the confused demon, just great.

Letting out another long groan, I rubbed at my aching temples. "You know, I'm not even going to get into it with you going through my phone right now because I do not have the time or the energy." I didn't bother looking at him when I spoke because I was just done with him right now. "Just... Leave me alone. I have a deadline I have to meet that I'm behind on."

I was not in the mood to edit right now, but I—

And leave it to Valphan's disdain to interrupt my train of thought. "Well, if you didn't waste your precious hours on those stupid men vying for attention who were obviously incompatible with you."

And there goes the boiling pot.

Sucking in a deep breath, I slowly turned my chair around to face him with a saccharine smile. "Is that jealousy I hear? That's not very befitting for such a high demon prince like you to be jealous of a mere human." Instead of explosive anger, I was seething and calm as I spoke to him. Those also weren't the words I wanted to throw at him either, but it would seem that I'd be procrastinating tonight. "Though, you've no one to blame for the icky green-eyed monster besides yourself."

Serves him right for going through my phone behind my back.

Scoffing, Valphan sat up straight and crossed his arms with a scowl on his face. "Well, I wouldn't be so offended if you didn't waste your time with trash like them. I mean, seriously? The man is forty and has no job or ambitions in life. Also, why on God's green earth are you going out with someone nearly twice your age who is literally going to go nowhere in life? Hm?"

"Oh, as if I'm better off with your ancient ass," I grumbled sardonically with a roll of my eyes.

"Excuse you?" Valphan snapped back with a mock offense.

"No, excuse you." I snarked, glaring at him softly. "I am nearly thirty, and he was only thirty-five." I corrected him with some sass and a scowl of my own. "And it's none of your business who I choose to entertain."

"It is very much my business because you are mine, so the only person you should be giving your attention and time to is me." Okay, maybe this little jealousy thing on him was kind of cute with how his face pouted with his glaring gray eyes. Annoying but slightly cute, just very slightly.

Crossing my arms, I leaned back in my seat with my legs crossed. "Oh, and like you're any better? Last I checked, you're an unemployed demon who lives in my closet." I quipped back with a smug smirk.

"Nah ah, correction cupcake, I am trapped in your closet. I do not choose to live in this place, but even if I did, it wouldn't be in a closet." Then, his face twisted with a cocky grin, baring his sharp teeth at me. "I'd be right in your bed next to you."

Letting out a frustrated scoff, I grabbed the first thing within reach—a spare pillow on my bed—and chucked it at Valphan with a grunt. "I will kick you to the floor," I grumbled with a soft glare.

Valphan's eyes sparkled with joy as he threw his head back in a hearty laugh. Then, with swift reflexes, he caught the large pillow before it could hit his face and held it close to his chest, sporting a wide smile on his lips. Stuffing his face into the soft surface, he rubbed into it while inhaling deeply—like I could literally hear him sniff my pillow!

Keeping his face obscured by the pillow, he spoke up. "Well, if I can have a pillow, then I'll be more than happy to sleep beside you like your mangy mutt." I barely made out his words because they were so muffled.

"You are so weird," I commented with a roll of my eyes as I watched Valphan snuggle the shit out of my pillow like a dog losing itself with its favorite blanket or bed.

Popping his head back up, he grins at me goofily as if he just smoked a whole bag of weed. "You smell sweet and homey, like burning firewood and caramel."

Okay, creepy and a little weird, a little specific, but I couldn't argue with him because it was kind of sweet with how much attention he paid. "W-well, I don't want it back now after you've got your demon cooties all over it, so it's yours now." Also, he seemed a little too happy, and as much as I wanted to punch him in the gut, I couldn't bring myself to ruin his little moment right now.

"Will you leave me alone to work if I let you keep the dang pillow?" I asked in a low voice while slowly turning back around to face my desk.

Keeping the overjoyed grin on his face, he curled up on the floor with the pillow tightly in his arms. "Yes, I will be content with watching you work in silence if that is what you need." Using his thin, pointed tail, he fetched one of the many blankets stored in my closet to lay over himself.

"Do you have to watch me?" I grumbled with a soft huff, doing my best to focus on the manuscript on the screen before me.

Nothing stuck, no matter how hard I tried to read the endless lines of text. Words came up off the screen and bounced right off me like rain to an umbrella. The pair of beady gray eyes out of my periphery weren't helping by any means—damn psycho demon.

"Is something the matter?" Does he ever shut up? "You've been staring at the same thing for longer than usual. Is it that bad?" If he wasn't stuck to an area around the closet, I'm pretty sure he'd be right over my shoulder right now like a petulant child.

Well, he may as well be with his damn shadow hands!

"Would you...!" Seething under my breath, I slapped at the annoying shadow replica of his hands that rested on my shoulders. "Quit touching me."

Pouting and whining softly, he sat up straight. "But you're tense. You need a good rub to relax." Wiggling the hands in the air didn't help the whole creepy vibe. Like, okay, maybe in a strange way, it was cute, and if I were in a better mood and in good standing with Valphan, then I'd tease him about it. But not when I was annoyed as hell with him.

"Touch me, and I will move to my living room to finish working," I threatened in a flat voice, staring my stern face at him to emphasize the seriousness of my threat.

Yeah, that got him to pull his shadow hands back into the closet. "No, stay. I won't touch you, promise." The kicked-puppy look on his demonic face should be illegal. Not because it was horrendous or anything. He looked too damn adorable to stay upset at.

He seriously made me feel like a villain with how dejected he looked over the next hour as I attempted to work again. It was bad enough that I almost caved and apologized to him. Too bad I was too stubborn and petty.

Begrudgingly, I gave out a displeased mutter before spinning my chair around a few times to try and release my stubborn knot before snapping my head over to Valphan. Cute idiot sat there staring at me with stars in his eyes, being so freaking patient like some saint. "My shoulders feel a little tight... Can you get the knots out?" I relented after a moment of struggling to get my words out. "Just quit looking like I killed your puppy," I muttered.

"Well, if that's all it takes, then I will forever look like this to get your sympathy." I wanted to wipe the wide grin off his face and take my words back, but it was too late now.

Well, I couldn't complain about the result. "Oh God, yes." Sighs and moans of pure pleasure heated my room up as I slumped back into my chair.

Valphan's face twisted in annoyance as he begged, "Don't say his name like that." Running a hand down his face, he let out a low, scoffing groaning. "Actually, don't ever say his name in any kind of way that has to do with pleasure. Seriously, what is up with you humans and moaning his name in vain like that during the worst moments?"

"What? You prefer I say yours?" I teased with a smug chuckle.

"It would be the best thing to ever grace my ears besides your voice, that would put lust demons to shame." Damn sweet talker. Something like that shouldn't sound as alluring as it did, but I couldn't help the heat from flooding my cheeks while my chest swelled with pride. "Your voice really is something else, my little blessing. Even the best choruses of angels would be nothing in your shadow. I would pick you over the sounds of the tormented souls any day, too."

"Uhh, thanks...?" Was that last part supposed to be a compliment? I mean, I know my voice wasn't the best or worst around, but being compared to tortured souls did not feel much like a good thing.

Probably sensing my confusion and discomfort, Valphan chuckled amusingly at me. "It is a good thing when it comes from a demon who can get off on the screams of suffering souls in the fields of punishment."

As if that made it all any better!

Rolling my eyes, I let out a drawn-out sigh as I let my head lull over his direction, connecting my lazy gaze with him. "Can't you make some kind of sweeter comparison? You were doing so well until the tortured souls part." I remarked with a breathy sneer.

"Aww, does my little pink princess like compliments and praises?" Valphan's voice softened and rose in pitch with his teasing words as he leaned his grinning face a little out of the closet.

"Oh, just hush and go back to rubbing my shoulders, Val."

"Whatever my little blessing wants."

Chapter 8

Valphan

~2 weeks later~

"Val! Open the doors up this instant!"

She could pound on the doors all she wanted, but I won't budge.

"Val! I know you're in there, and you can hear me! So, open up!" Funny, she actually sounded a little mad with how strained her voice came out, along with the grunts and groans. "Val! You're going to make me late!"

Satisfied with my little sabotage, I crossed my arms behind my head as I continued to lounge in my makeshift bed. "Good." I raised my voice slightly to ensure it carried through the shut doors that jiggled violently from her struggles.

A frustrated outcry followed by a stomp vibrated the floor, causing me to laugh a little as I held the closet doors shut using my shadows. "You little asshole! I take back what I said about you yesterday. You're a jerk!" A loud thud jolted the wooden doors following her words. "Goldie is so much cuter and better than you! And he's a better cuddler! And at least he can give me kisses!"

Oh, that does it!

My irritation slammed against my ribcage so hard, along with the gust of the closet doors being thrown open, that I nearly winded myself. "You're going to regret that," I growled as shadow hands shot out and wrapped themselves around her limbs, yanking her right into my arms.

Unbridled lust stormed my body like invaders to a castle the moment I wrapped my arms around her pear-shaped body and pressed her softness right up against me. With an arm tightly around her waist and lower back, I move the other against her back, pressing the full length of it against her slender spine as I grab the back of her head. "I will kiss every inch of your body until nothing is left untouched after I claim this smartass mouth of yours," I growled against her lips before kissing her roughly, bullying my tongue into her mouth while holding her protestant head as still as possible.

Fuck, she tasted so divine and unholy. Like the earthy soils of home after fresh snow has dusted it, and like the fresh snow itself. The kind of snow from home that was made of suffering and tears. She also tasted forbidden, like the fruit Eden bit into after giving into temptation.

Sweet mother Lilith.

I was addicted.

Mind-numbing bliss shattered with my muffled grunt of pain. Instinctively, I reeled back at the sudden sting around my tongue akin to a guillotine. "Mother—" Hissing in pain, I let go of her head to hold my bleeding mouth.

Boiling anger from having my tongue attacked by her teeth simmered out to thrilling arousal as my lips pulled into a dark, bloody grin. Amused, I watched her pull her hand back and swing it at me, only to be stopped by a shadow tendril before her open palm could sting my cheek.

Her body tightened against mine with a grunt from the shadow tendrils pulling taut. With her limbs tied down, I grabbed her face and forced her to tilt her head so I could have access to her succulent neck. Leaning in, I pressed my injured tongue against her innocent skin, tainting it with a streak of my saliva and blood as I licked up her throbbing artery to her cheek. "Maybe I might just let you go on that stupid date," my voice dropped lower and lower as I got to her ear, "After I mark you as mine."

Her eyes went as wide as her stupid dinner plates at my words, causing a small wave of laughter to below out of my shaking chest. "What is my little blessing thinking to have such a face?" Well, I had some good guesses, but I didn't mean anything *too* dirty by my words.

"Y-you touch in any way without my permission, and I will move out and light this place up as I walk out." Her voice may tremble, but her threat was stern, along with her hardened eyes that chilled my spine.

Letting go of her face, I held my hands up in surrender while leaning back slightly. "I'm a demon, not someone with no morals." Okay, that was better in my head, but it was true!

Sputtering out a laugh, Gracie struggled to reel herself back in with some coverup coughs. "You want to repeat what you just said? Maybe a little louder so it gets through your old ears?"

Rolling my eyes, I reached out and flicked her forehead. "I ain't into non-consensual stuff, especially with someone who's a virgin." If her limbs weren't restrained, she probably would have reeled back and placed a hand on her chest with her exaggerated sigh of offense. "Oh, don't you get all prude with me now, little Prudence. I can smell your innocence as much as I can feel it, your soul and aura, I mean." If I were daring enough, then technically, I could stick something up there and violate her, but I wasn't that kind of demon.

She let out a seething breath and puffed her angry cheeks out with a displeased growl. "Don't call me that!" She snapped with a deep scowl.

"I mean, if that were my name, then I wouldn't want anyone calling me it either." Seriously, did her parents hate her? I wonder how badly she was bullied for her name growing up.

Gracie thrashed against her restraints. "Well...! Well...! Ugh!" The way she pressed her lips into a tight line meant I'd won this round.

Or so I thought. "Well, at least I don't look like a dog or a little baby deer, Fawny."

Okay, a little offended, not gonna lie because, well, "What the fuck?" Okay, maybe I misheard because, "What. The. Fucking. Finest. Pardon."

"You're a little Fawn." Cocky little thing even dared to stick her tongue out at me.

"Woman, are you high out of your unholy mind?" Did she have a fall I was unaware of? Get hit in the head when she went out grocery shopping earlier? Rotted her brain away with all her manuscript editing?

"You look like Goldie, and he has a fawn coat," Gracie remarked with a sneer and puff of her chest.

Yep, really offended now. "Did you just put me on the same level as your mutt? The one who chases his own tail and licks his own ass?" Or maybe I was hallucinating or caught in a very bad nightmare because in no way in this limbo realm did my own mate just equate me to her dog. Albeit a cute dog, I'll give the thing that much credit, but not a hair more.

Still offended. I mean, I looked way cuter and better than a dog by eons. Also, I had more brains than a dog, so was she insinuating that I was also stupid with her comparison?

"How on earth do I—" Cutting myself off, I shook my head with a dismissive wave of my hand, "Never mind, I don't want to know."

Shoving my irritations out of my mind, I grabbed her face to bring her into another kiss, wanting to lose myself in her intoxicating freshness again. Breaking away briefly to let her breathe, I glared softly into her eyes, "You are not going on that useless date." I grumbled against her lips with a deep growl and scowl. "You step out of this closet, out that door, and you will not be sleeping tonight."

Slipping my hand into her dye locks, which were surprisingly very soft, I gripped them tightly to tilt her head up at me. "And make no mistake, my words are no threat or warning. They are a promise." Leaning her back, I loomed over her menacingly. "Just because I am nice doesn't mean I do not have a mean bone in my body. I may sweeten you with words that light up your face like a sunny day, but those words can easily light a different kind of fire within you along with my touch."

Make no mistake, the thought of cherishing her in my arms, snuggling in bed, having her in my lap while she worked, all of that was lovely, but I had my baser needs, which darkened my lustful thoughts about my beautiful mate. The need to hold her down and make her scream for all of Heaven and Hell to hear stiffened every—and I do mean every—inch of me with a burning desire for her.

Oh, the things I will do to you once you kneel to me, my little blessing.

That thought caused another flurry of sinful images to cross my mind.

Pressing my smirking lips against her in a sensual kiss, I chuckled softly. "Well? What's your choice, little blessing? Out? Or in?"

Tauntingly, I had a shadow hand pick up the outfit she'd set out for the night and waved it in the air like a flag.

"Choose wisely for the sake of being able to walk and think straight tomorrow."

Chapter 9
Gracie

I DON'T THINK I chose wisely.

Pretty sure if I did, then I wouldn't be hesitant about entering my room, where Valphan stood at the closet door, crowding the opening with his menacing grin while beckoning me toward him with a clawed finger.

Swallowing the nervous lump in my throat, I glued my feet to the floor right outside the door to my room. Steeling my nerves, I defiantly shook my head at him while shaking in my panties.

I had no one but myself to blame for this situation because Valphan gave me two very clear options. Stupidly, just to spite him, I picked the one that involved me wasting a few hours of my life with another man who did nothing but disappoint me. Yeah, those few hours could have been better spent at home on my computer, or hell, it would have been better wasted on Valphan.

"Come on, my little pink princess," he cooed with the most twisted, fang-bearing smile ever, "You can't stand there forever."

"Yes, I can," I remarked defiantly with a stomp of my foot and a scowl.

Then, an idea crossed my mind, causing my lips to curl upward. "Actually, I think I need to break in the guest bed, make sure it's nice and slept in."

Seeing the way Valphan's lips pressed into a tight, flat line made mine widen with victory.

Two can play at this game.

"Well, goodnight, Fawny!" I teased with an overabundant giggle, turning on my heel with the extra effect of a hair flick in his direction.

Instead of forward, I found my body moving backward, with a shriek erupting from my throat. My ass hit the hard floor with a winded grunt before my body was dragged over to my doom.

With my back pressed flat against the ground, the shadow hands practically chained me to the ground right outside the closet. The soft light from the lamp in my room darkened with Valphan's shadow as he stepped over me like a conqueror would over his victim to be killed. "Oh, it'll definitely be a good night for me." His voice sounded deeper and sinister from down here, causing me to shiver and gasp.

Panic and excitement chased each other through my body the more I shrunk under Valphan's dark gaze while struggling against my restraints, which were rather soft. Strangely, they felt like soft leather bindings against my silky-smooth skin. It was odd to me because usually, his shadows felt rougher, harder, sometimes as hard as steel, while other times they felt almost like flesh.

His leather pants creaked with his slow downward lean to hover his face inches above mine. The moonlight streaming in from the window and the lamp's light bounced off his gnarly fangs as he grinned excitedly at me. "The only thing that will be broken in tonight, is you."

Words escaped with my sharp gasp from the suddenness of my dress being torn off my body by his clawed hand. "H-hey! That dress was expensive." And I liked it too.

"I'll get you a new one if it bothers you that much." He commented with a roll of his eyes before kissing me deeply with a small groan. "Can't wait to see your juicy ass shake with your body while you come." His hot words washed over my shivering lips as I felt my legs spreading and bending at the knees with some force from the tendrils.

His words sent chills down to my soul, making my body tense as my panic kicked my body into a fight or flight mode from the thought of having my virginity taken away in a crude manner like this. "Valphan, please, I don't want to have sex." Desperation dripped off every pleading word as I looked at him wide-eyed. My chest heaved with my quickened breaths as I nervously laid there helplessly spread before him in nothing but my bra and matching panties.

Frowning softly, Valphan reached and stroked my face tenderly while shushing me. "I will do no such thing tonight or any other night, not until you beg me to make you bleed with my cock and willingly spread your legs wide for me like the good girl you are deep down." How the hell could he sound so sweet but crude and hot at the same time like that? It wasn't fair. I should be totally creeped out and turned off by that, not shuddering and getting wet at the thought of whatever monstrosity he hid in his pants claiming my innocent body.

"W-well, I don't want you touching me! You don't have my consent to lay a single finger on me." Surely, I thought that would have been the end since he said he wasn't one to do something without consent. Yet, he only smiled warmly at me briefly as he studied my face like an artist would their model.

Then, his smile softened into a devilish smirk as he sat back against the closet door frame with his arms loosely crossed. "As you wish, my Gracie." He didn't budge one bit as he sat there smugly.

Now, I expected to feel the pressure ease off my limbs, for my body to be free to tackle and beat his ass, but no. The little movement that did happen was only for a pillow and a few blankets to be slipped under me for some makeshift bed, but then it was back on the ground, still spread wide and trapped by these stupid shadow tendrils!

"Fawny, I swear, if you don't release me this instant." My voice trailed out with my nonexistent threat hanging on my tongue. I couldn't do jack shit tied down like this, and I couldn't free myself, not unless Valphan allowed it.

"Va-aaah!" The feeling of something rubbing against my covered sex made me flinch and yelp from the increasing pressure.

Reluctantly, I bucked my hips away, well, tried to. I didn't have much wiggle room with how firm the shadows kept me locked down, and when I tried to move my hips away, a thick rope of shadow wrapped itself around my waist and hip to keep it still. Craning my head up, I winced at the burning stretch biting the back of my neck. "Valphan! Don't touch me!" I spat at him through gritted teeth.

Fuck.

The wooden floors creaked with pain as my nails scraped against them from my fingers and toes curling. Pleasure bloomed from my core as a result of a shadow hand stroking the length of my sex from top to bottom with the occasional circling of my aching clit.

It was hard not to enjoy this, and I felt a little guilty for it. But... I needed it. It had been a while since I gave myself a release.

No! No! Do not get off from a freaking shadow!

Fighting the tides of pleasure washing over my body, I threw my head back down against the pillow, groaning a bit from the soft thud of the impact. "I told you not to touch me!" I strained out through my clenched jaw.

The air warmed with his amused laughter. "And I am not."

Peering around my bent leg, I scoffed and rolled my eyes at the sight of his relaxed and arrogant face. Tension scrunched my face up until I was scowling and glaring at the damn demon. "Yes, you are." I bit out with emphasis on each word.

Sighing softly, as if this whole thing were a joke to him, he began to fiddle around with the waistband of his pants. "As you can clearly see, I am sitting quite a ways from you, and in no way is any part of my body in contact with you."

Fucking smartass.

What happened next had my eyes going so wide that I thought they'd pop out of my head. His roaring laughter blurred into the background because I was too horrified at the sight of his dick—his inhuman dick!

Okay, I probably shouldn't be shocked because Stella told me about Kastoron's tool below and how it wasn't normal. She also went into great detail about his size and how it looked. Honestly, I probably shouldn't be as shocked as I am right now, but hearing about demon dick and then actually seeing one was a totally different ball game.

Also, Valphan's dick looked *nothing* like Kastoron's from what Stella's described. I think she said Kastoron's was lined with ridges, which was definitely not the case with Valphan. Dude was huge; that part was accurate. I mean, it was hard to judge from the slight distance, but pretty sure he was the size of my forearm. Ten inches, maybe twelve? Longer? Either way, he was long and thick with a thick ass mushroom head as a tip. Now, the size wasn't what got me *too* much; it was the build.

His fucking penis was bumpy as shit! Long rows of bumps, all varying in sizes, stretched from his tip down to his base in a wavy line. Yeah, if it wasn't attached to him, then it could pass as an exotic toy or a fetish toy, but the fact it was real really tripped me up.

"Like what you see, cupcake?" Valphan teased me with a loud laugh as he took ahold of his member in his large hand after spitting into it and stroked it slowly before my very eyes.

Words and saliva pooled in my needy mouth as I stared shamelessly at him, lazily stroking himself. I was too stunned to think of anything good to throw back at him. If anything, I'd make a damn fool of myself if I opened my mouth and drooled like a starving dog staring at a bone.

"If you want it, then all you have to do is beg for it." The way his taunting words dipped so lowly with his darkening gaze sent a wave of arousal through my heightened body, causing me to squirm in my spot while my pussy clenched around nothing in need.

Shutting my eyes tight, I forced myself to turn away from the temptation. "It won't fit." I whimpered, letting the fear of the thing impaling me and ripping me apart send my mind back to reality. "You'll kill me if you put that thing inside of me."

Apparently, he must have thought it funny because he bellowed a laugh that shook the room. "Your friend and Kastoron are alive and well, and no doubt he fucks her as much as I'm going to fuck you." Rolling his eyes, Valphan slouched a little as the sounds of him pleasuring himself continued to fill the room. "There are spells of protection to make it possible for you to take me and not break. Don't worry about such trivial things. I'll take care of you from start to finish and beyond."

Okay, I had to give him some credit for his last words. They were teeth rotting sweet to me. Fucking melted my resistance like chocolate on a stovetop. Damn demon, how dare he be so fucking smooth.

No! No. Don't give in. Just bear through it. He'll get bored and release you eventually.

Staring up at my ceiling, I tried my best to lose myself by counting the popcorn. Unfortunately, Valphan didn't let that happen.

A sharp gasp straightened my spine at the sound of clothes ripping and the feeling of cold air hitting my wet, throbbing cunt. "Valphan!" I squeaked in protest as I instinctively tried to close my legs to keep myself decent.

Shudders raked my body at the smooth sound of Valphan's deep chuckle. "My, my, what a lovely cunt you have, my mate. So plump and perfectly wet, just begging to be stuffed full." I could hear his deep groan and his breath picking up in pace. "You're going to look so divine stretched tight around my cock."

Now, I couldn't help myself from letting out a moan of my own as my mind flashed with images of my legs spread wide and him on top of me. The phantom feeling of him bullying my tight walls with his thickness had my hips bucking at the shadow hand, rubbing my cunt for more friction as my body burned needily for him.

My hardened nipples scraped against the fabric of my bra with each heave of my chest. With each rub of the shadow hand, combined with the fantasies in my mind and stimulated nipples, my orgasm piqued faster than I anticipated. The telltale sign of my stomach turning into knots caught me off guard because of how fast it came on, and before I knew it, I was—

"Fuck! No!"

Frustrated as fuck.

Chapter 10

Valphan

WOW, SHE WAS MUCH more stubborn than I credited her for.

If I read the clock on the wall right, she'd been holding out for a good hour and a half. For an inexperienced person, she handled being edged so well. Granted, she verbally let me know about her frustration.

"Ugh! You asshole!" Weakly, she lifted her head up to glare at me momentarily before throwing her head back with a groan when the shadow hand pressed back against her swollen sex.

The only torturous part of this, for me, was not being able to touch her myself. Yeah, I could feel a little through my shadows, but merely a ghost feeling. I wanted to put my hands on her, feel the softness of her glowing skin as her body would writhe under me with pleasure brought on by my body. To be able to press my fingers into her wetness, spread her slick juices around as I would explore every inch and dip of her delicious cunt from her outer lips to her entrance. Oh, I bet her soft, tight walls would feel more perfect than home.

Biting back my groan of desire, I stopped stroking myself for a second to recollect myself. Resisting her became harder by the second the more her sweet, musky scent invaded my system, along with the sounds of her wet, plump pussy lips being rubbed. And sweet Lucifer, her hellish moans, so fucking lovely. I was tempted to bring her to orgasm once or twice just to keep her sweet melodies going until she screamed with pleasure from the effects of her orgasm breaking at every fiber of her being.

Hissing out a cuss under my breath, I forced the shadow hand away from her bucking hips when her moaning and breathing picked up in pace, along with her tensing body.

With a frustrated cry, she smacked the ground with an open palm. "No!" She shouted in protest with an angry glare at me. "You jerk face! Let me come!" She demanded rather rudely.

Drifting my eyes down her lovely body, I took my sweet time running my eyes over the subtle curves and soft rolls of her waist to the flare of her wide hips, which led to her big, bubbly ass squished out under her. And fuck! Those thighs! I wanted to snuggle my face into them so badly and sleep my life away on them. Forcing my eyes back to hers, I offered her a rather smug smirk, "Not if that's the tone you're using." I drew out a lazy sigh as I went back to stroking my aching member.

Snapping at me with a growl, she turned her attention away from me again as her back arched with a loud, tortured moan from my shadow hand, stimulating her again. "I can keep this up all night, princess." I taunted her with a laugh, briefly increasing the pressure of the hand to give her a nice kick before pulling back, causing her to let out another angry whine.

Again and again, her moans ebbed and waned with her rising and plummeting pleasure from my constant edging. Honestly, I could do and watch this all night because it was more than entertaining to me. Seeing the way her body glowed with her sheen of sweat while it trembled from the impending orgasm and seeing the way her eyes filled with bliss and hope as her pleasure crept towards the edge—lovely. But what I loved more was the way her body would freeze up and drop while the promise in her eyes shattered to pure disappointment and anger.

She was close to breaking, though. I could feel it and see it. Just a little more, and she'd be begging me to no end. Her eyes were so blown wide with need that they almost looked black instead of their usual brown, and I could see the fight in her body shed each time I brought her right up to the edge of pleasure just to take it away before such bliss could grace her senses. And with each lift and drop, her words slowly faded to mere moans, groans, gasps, and grunts.

Standing up with a soft sigh, I walked over to her and loomed over her panting body. "Come on, you know what you have to do, my little blessing. Why do you keep torturing yourself?"

Gracie couldn't even muster up a full response, sputtering nonsensical sounds at me while her eyes pleaded desperately with me. If I was a little nicer, I would have given in to her big, doe-like eyes right then and there. Too bad I could be just as stubborn as her. "What do you need, my little pink princess?" Hopefully, some of my words would be enough to get a coherent answer.

"Come. Need. Come. Please." She struggled to pronounce her words clearly through her heavy, whimpering breaths.

Unable to help myself, I smiled deviously down at her as I squatted next to her head and stroked myself inches from her pouty lips. "You need my cum? Or do you need to come?" Okay, now I was just being an asshole to her, but I really couldn't let this opportunity pass.

Now, I expected some kind of frustrated groan or a scowl of some sort with a glare from her, so her answer threw me a bit for a loop. "Both, please." Greedy little thing she was, apparently.

I kinda felt bad when she started to lift her head and craned her neck toward my cock so needily and when she stuck her tongue out as far as it would go for a taste, only to stop less than an inch from me, yeah, that knocked down my hard wall.

"You know what you have to do, cupcake." I mused with a drawn-out sigh.

Clenching her jaw, she shut her eyes tightly for a brief moment before relenting with the next orgasm denial from my shadow hand. "Valphan, please, I can't take it anymore, please! I need to come, please! Please! Please touch me, kiss me, bite me, scratch me, taint my body with your hellish one. I don't care what you do to me. Just please, make me come." I was surprised she got that all out in one breath.

The thought of taking her fully right here and now circled around my mind like a tempting snake on my shoulders, but I forced it away out of respect for my mate. She may be begging me to let her come, make her come, to lay my hands on her, but she also said earlier not to have sex with her. Additionally, she was not of sound mind right now, so I didn't want to take things too far and cross a road we would never be able to come back from.

Letting go of myself, I steadied myself with a hand on the floor as I leaned down closer. Grabbing her face with the other hand, I forced her to extend her neck as far as possible to bring her into a lip-crushing kiss. "Let me take care of you first," I muttered against her lips before kissing my way down her body, snapping her bra off on the way down.

Settling between her legs, I dismissed the shadow hand from her sex, having it rest against her inner thigh instead. The air in her room was thick with her scent, but being inches from her sweet cunt, oh, Lucifer. I didn't think her scent could be more potent, but hellish lord, my mind was becoming drunk off her strong scent as I moved in on her.

Peering up at her, I kept my observant eyes locked on her reactions, wanting to catch every little twist and twitch of her sweet face as she'd watch me feast upon her cunt. The corners of my lips curved into a smirk as my long, thick tongue slithered out of my mouth to lick the full length of her cunt with an eye-rolling moan the instant her sweet nectar bathed my tastebuds.

Fuck. I was hooked.

Sealing my lips around her, I pressed my full tongue against her swollen clit, giving it a languid lick and a soft suck while I dipped the tip of my tongue past her entrance. Her poor body froze under me with her jagged gasp as her hips bucked at me. "Oh, fuck, more, please, more." The sweetness of her pleas made my resolve melt away like ice to a fire, and my painful cock twitched with a need to stuff itself into her warmth.

Growling softly, I wrapped my arms around her thighs to anchor her fully against me before digging into her like a starved demon. With how much I've edged her, it only took a few swipes of my tongue and movements of my head to push her right back to the edge of her orgasm. Now, my twisted side wanted to edge her again, just once, for shit and giggles, but I couldn't do that to her after seeing her doe eyes filled with so much wanton.

So, I took her to Hell.

Her moans picked up in pitch and volume until she screamed full-on with joy. "Oh fuck! Valphan!" Her scream shook my body along with the air in the room, and I wouldn't be surprised if her neighbors heard her.

Instead of easing off once she reached her peak, I pressed on until her eyes turned white from rolling back so far. Then, her head fell back with her spasming body. "Fuckfuckfuckfuck." She sputtered helplessly as her body fell to my mercy.

Like a juicy apple, I sucked and licked at every inch of her, not letting any drop of her juices escape me. As I enjoyed my meal, Gracie surprised me with a very nice mouthful to quench my growing thirst for her. My little mate squealed and sobbed under me as her body shook from the pleasure and overstimulation I brought upon her.

Over and over, I brought her body to a string of endless orgasms through her pleas for me to take it easy on her and give her a break. But no, I wanted her to break from the pleasure. Pleasure *I* gave her. I wanted to ruin her for everyone else so she'd be forced to turn to me for relief.

I didn't slow to a stop until she was a delirious moaning mess. The makeshift blanket mattress under her was completely soaked from all her squirting and gushing that I—shamefully—failed to lap up by the time I broke my latch from her twitching cunt. Poor thing was so sensitive that she nearly screamed when I pressed a kiss against her overstimulated sex and chuckled softly.

Sitting back on my knees, I stared down at her in awe. Like the finest demoness, and dare I say, an ethereal angel, her stunning body shone under the pale light of the moon streaming through her window from her sheen of sweat. Her petite breasts swelled with every rise of her chest as she panted heavily in her post-orgasmic haze. Then, her sweet face, covered in tears and drool, stretched out in the most blissful smile I've ever seen.

I always found tears amusing and arousing, being a torturer in the endless frozen tundra of Hell. Bringing people to tears by inflicting pain and other kinds of suffering was as easy and natural as breathing. Yet, never before have I brought someone to tears through orgasms, mainly because I never had the inkling need for it. Now, though, after seeing Gracie's beautiful face stained with her tears of bliss, I may have found a new addiction.

Leaning over my lovely mate, I moved my head to meet her blown eyes, causing them to twitch as she struggled to focus on me. "You look so fucking lovely right now." If only I could capture this moment to keep forever.

Cupping her face with a blissful smile of my own, I stroked her cheek with my thumb as I looked at her tenderly. "I've never loved tears so much until seeing them stain your plush cheeks, my little blessing."

With a smile, I leaned down and kissed her deeply, engaging in a deep and heated make-out session with her for a few moments.

"I am going to make you cry every morning and night from pleasure."

Chapter 11

Gracie

I HAD THE BEST dream last night and the best orgasm, err orgasms, in my life. It was so wild and amazing that I didn't care if it was Valphan in my dream. I'd been so pent up the past few weeks with no time or energy to use any of my toys to relieve myself because I would knock out the moment my head hit the pillow, and the warmth of Valphan's shadowy embrace held me in bed.

Yeah, my little closet demon probably thought he was slick with slipping his shadows under the sheets with me every night. I stopped trying to get him to quit the habit after it was obvious he wouldn't. Also, I noticed how he'd wait until I was completely asleep or close to falling deep before holding me with his shadows—I caught him a few times when I pretended to sleep to test the theory out.

But none of that mattered right now. I was too blissful and comfortable in my soft blanket cocoon to care about anything related to Valphan and his stubbornness right now.

On cloud nine, I was about ready to fall back asleep until the sounds of scrapping echoing down the hallway caused me to bolt upright in my bed, clutching my sheets tightly against my—

Oh my God, I'm naked, what the fuck!?

Okay, now I was thoroughly confused because I came home from—

A lumpy pile out of the corner of my eyes made me dart my head over to the area outside my closet. "Oh my God." Slapping a hand over my gasping mouth, I stared at the bundle of messed-up blankets with a pillow off to the side of it.

It didn't hit me before, but now, as I stared in horror at the 'bed' Valphan took me on last night, the phantom scent of our activities filled my nostrils. Memories churned around in my mind, playing last night at the forefront of my mind; it was as if I was in a movie theater watching my 'dream' in fucking 3D.

"Don't worry, I'll clean it all up." And as if I wasn't stunned enough this morning, hearing Valphan's voice come somewhere, not the closet, caused me to let out a startled scream as my body jolted to face my door.

"Jumpy little thing, aren't you, pinkie." Valphan laughed softly as he entered the room with a plate of food in one hand and a big glass of orange juice in the other.

Needless to say, seeing my closet demon serve me breakfast in bed when he was supposed to be stuck in the closet after a mind-blowing orgasmic night confused the shit out of me. "Wha? Huh?" Honestly, I thought I was still dreaming or possibly hallucinating.

Unbothered by my reaction, Valphan sat next to me at the edge of the bed. "Isn't this usually where you get all lovey-dovey and thank me? Or are those stories of yours really that inaccurate to life nowadays?" He asked while setting the glass of orange juice down on my nightstand before picking up a piece of bacon and holding it up to my lips. "Eat. You need to replenish after last night, and no, the chocolate and cold meat I fed you and your crackers don't count for much after you slept off all of it."

Completely shell-shocked, all I could do was obey him, munching away at the piece of bacon and all the other pieces of food he fed me like a mindless robot. It was strange to be fed by my closet demon, but it was very sweet and nice. I've never been spoiled like this before; I've only ever read about it in fiction stories or heard about it from people who had marriages made in Heaven.

"Is something the matter, cupcake?" Valphan's concern forced me out of my head to give my full attention to him.

"I..." Zipping my lips, I shook my head to clear it before something stupid came out. "Last night... Did that really all happen?" It still didn't feel real to me, even though the evidence was literally right there. "We didn't... You didn't fuck me after, right?"

I felt a little sore down there, but not to the point where it felt like I wouldn't be able to walk, which I figured would be the case if he did screw me stupid with his demon dick.

Wait! Oh my God, his dick!

Craziness took over me for the next few seconds as I scrambled to Valphan on my hands and knees. Grabbing the waistband of his pants, I pulled it away from his body to look down at his nether regions. "Holy shit, it's real." I gasped with bugging eyes as I shamelessly stared at his flaccid cock in utter shock. Yeah, it didn't look as menacing as last night because it was soft, but it still had some size and bulk to it, and I could see its bumpy texture.

A soft puff of air smacked my face from his pants snapping back to his body after he snatched my hand away. "What happened to asking for permission first?" His voice teased my blushing face from above with a hearty chuckle. "Not that I will ever mind my mate looking at what is hers. I thought you were a little too prude to be grabbing at people like that."

And sweet moment over.

Shoving my embarrassment away, I pulled myself away and hid myself under my covers. "Go away." I stammered out.

"Only because I have to put things into the washer, which, by the way, is so much better than washing things by hand." He mused as I felt the bed ease.

Confused, I peeped my head out to watch him move over to last night's mess and gather up the sheets. "You're going to wash them? Not complaining or anything, but I can do it later."

Waving his tail at me, he merely glanced back at me as he made his way to the door. "Cupcake, I made you make this mess, and it was my idea in the first place, so it's my job to take care of the aftermath." Okay, his happy little grin melted my racing heart. "The only thing I want you to do is rest and worry about meeting your deadlines. Let me worry about all the little nuances around your life."

"W-wait, we need to talk though." About a lot of shit.

"We will." He assured me with a confident smile. "After I throw these into your machine and run you a bath."

"Huh?" I never said or mentioned anything about a bath. Or was that his somewhat subtle way of saying I reek? "Why do I need a bath?" That came out a little more cold and accusatory than I intended, but it was out now.

Laughing softly, he looked at me with intrigued eyes for a second before replying. "Because you have a shit ton of those little bath bombs that need to be used up, and you need to be spoiled." That was a strange answer, and I wondered if that was a coverup for the truth. "You smell just fine. I'm not wanting to clean you because you reek of sex from last night." He quickly held a hand up to stop the words from coming from my open mouth. "And no, I cannot read your mind, yet you just have that stupid look on your face like you're offended."

Now I felt like throwing something at him for being right. "Do you know how to use the laundry machines?"

From what I've found out the past few weeks with him, he knew nothing about the modern world. Granted, he was a fast learner, and contact with his demon friends quickly caught him up a bit. Still, he may have the knowledge, but experience-wise, not so much since he was confined to the closet until now.

Actually, now that I thought about it, how was my house not on fire from him making breakfast? I mean, stoves weren't *that* hard to figure out, but still, he could have turned on the wrong knob or left something on and let the gas leak. Good news was that I didn't smell any gas.

"Yes, the others taught me how when I contacted them. Don't worry. I won't be breaking any of your stuff." With a flash of a reassuring smile, Valphan wagged his thin tail at me with a sassy flick before he disappeared completely out of my room.

I must admit, as strange as this all was, it was nice. However, I couldn't help but feel anxious thinking about our conversation last night once he came back. Well, the impending conversation about our relationship going forward really got my nerves on edge.

People don't go back to being buddies after a night like that. Yeah, he's claimed and said numerous times that I was his mate, a claim I've shot down and rejected myself because the notion of it was crazy to me. Also, it felt like a cop-out for a relationship. To be together because we were destined.

As much as I wanted someone to love me in life, I didn't want it to be handed on a platter and be complacent with it. I wanted to be wooed, courted the fuck out of, and trip head over heels for my lover. I didn't want to be a match, said, and done.

Yes, I wanted my relationship to be one of those cheesy, lovey, dopey romance stories I edit time in and time out, like the story I was writing myself as my debut as a published author. Call me a hopeless romantic, but I wanted my love story to be teeth-rotting sweet and spicy like the world's hottest pepper, the ones that instantly have your body on fire to the point where you have to strip and cool off however you can.

"Little blessing? What is on your mind?" Valphan's voice snapped me out of my trance once he reentered the room and sat beside me on the bed.

Sighing heavily, I dragged a tired hand through my bedhead. "Too much... I don't know where to start with us and everything." Groaning softly, I let my hand fall down my face as I stared into space.

The sounds of fabric shuffling along with the soft hit of cold air from my covers being lifted cause me to recenter on reality.

Slipping under the covers, Valphan pulled me into his lap by my waist, and then he snuggled me tightly with a content smile and hum. "You have no idea how long I've wanted to do this ever since I saw you that first day. To be able to hold you in my arms right now feels like a dream come true." Groaning softly, he nuzzles his face into my hair and neck. "The amount of times I've toyed with the idea of dragging you into the closet to trap you in my arms is more than I care to admit."

"Why didn't you?" He could do such, and last night was a good example of him forcing me into the closet.

"Because I'm not a monster." He replied with a soft huff.

Staying silent for a moment, Valphan breathed me in deeply before sitting up straight against my headboard to look down at me with a strong smile and eyes full of determination. "I may want you more than anything in all the realms, but I also want your reciprocation. I will not force a relationship on you, soulmate or not. I want you to come to accept me and everything with time." Leaning down, he pressed his forehead against mine. "So, even if it means spending forever at your heel like your little mutt, then I will gladly wag my little tail and be at your feet every second of every damn day as long as it means getting you to fall more and more for me until you can't resist me anymore."

"What if I never want you after all that time?" Impossible, but I had to pose the slight possibility.

The thought of being with a demon for the rest of my life seemed daunting, but the more time I spent around Valphan, the more of this strange pull I felt toward him. He may be a creepy, annoying little shit with how he constantly watched me while sitting at the closet entrance, but that was growing on me, slowly.

I could have easily set up my office in one of the other rooms and gotten some peace, but when I thought about doing it, the thought of not having his presence around or his adoring eyes to glimpse at when I needed a break gutted me a little. His creeping has become a comfort of sorts, a safety net. Also, he was a good backseat editor, even if that got annoying quickly; he caught a lot of little nuances I tend to miss regarding certain positioning and things with spice scenes.

His little shadowy touches also grew on me; they weren't inappropriate. They were innocent touches ranging from a hand on the shoulder to arms around my waist and hands on my thighs. If I didn't think much about it, it was no different than having a boyfriend hold me and touch me while I worked.

"Not possible, but I'd still follow you and stay by your side until death." Valphan didn't seem too offended or upset at the question. If anything, he sounded sure things were not happening.

Then, the urge to slap him hit me hard when Valphan smirked smugly at me. "And if last night was any indication of things headed in any direction, I say my chances are good." He snickered softly, leaning in and nipping at my neck playfully.

And, of course, that brought up the matter of last night.

Sighing heavily, I shifted around in his lap until I straddled him and faced him fully. "Last night... We... You never answered my question about us having sex." I fumbled my question out while rubbing the back of my neck a little raw.

Chuckling, Valphan wrapped his arms loosely around my waist, settling his hand at the top of my ass cheeks. "Well, considering how you can still move, I'd say I didn't do a good job if we did make love to each other." He joked with a hearty laugh, earning a few slaps on the chest from me and a soft glare.

Arousal tingled along my body in response to his finger stroking the swell of my bottom cheeks. "Cupcake, you told me no sex, so I was merely respecting your wishes." Bumping his forehead against mine, he forced my gaze to his tender smile. "You weren't in your right mind when you begged me to touch you and give you a release, so I didn't want to take advantage of your heightened state to take you fully."

... Okay, that was too fucking sweet. How the hell is a *demon* more damn respectful than people in this world? I assure you if I were to fall into the same situation with anyone else, there is a 90% chance they would have taken full advantage of me and then some.

Wow, what a world and time to live in where a demon is better than a human.

Taking in a deep breath, I let my eyes fall down his body, letting myself get lost in the contours of his muscles. At least he wasn't too bad looking for a demon. I mean, looking past the oddly ashen grey skin that was almost sickly pale and the horns... And the claws... He was actually pretty handsome. His body was like a perfect sculpture at the museum, not too bulky, not too lean, just perfectly average. Yeah, he was muscular and built, but it was almost more of an athletic build than a buffed-out bodybuilder.

Slowly, I could feel my cheeks tighten with the spread of my lips as the image of him sleeping on his little makeshift bed in my closet painted itself at the forefront of my mind.

Looking over, I could see his neatly made floor bed at the closet entrance, which consisted of my spare blankets and pillows and his all-time favorite, a brindle-colored faux fur blanket.

A gentle turn of my head focused my gaze back on my curious demon. "What's got you smiling?" He inquired with a raise of his eyebrow.

"Your bed, like always." I giggled softly, sticking my tongue out at him. "Are you still going to use it now that you're free from your closet prison?"

The thought of not being able to see him curled and bundled up made my smile sad. It was one of those moments I've come to enjoy from him. A peaceful sight to get lost in during my stressful times or late nights working away on manuscripts, and it was a cute sight to wake up to in the middle of the night. The countless images I've taken of him in such moments would live on my phone forever, but it wasn't the same. Looking at a picture of him didn't bring on the full warmth of appreciation, nor did I feel the entire weight of the gravitational pull toward him.

Much to my surprise, his smile turned melancholic as his gaze drifted to the closet. "That will still be my place at the end of the day." His somber tone weighed the air around us. "I am not completely free, just mere moments."

I should be glad that I'd still have my peace from him, that he didn't have free roam over my whole life, but the only thing I could feel was my heart sinking into the deepest pits of my stomach. "What do you mean?" I asked with a deep sigh after I leaned into him and settled myself against his bare chest.

Laying his head atop mine, he strokes my hair with one hand. "I'm on a tight leash to keep it as simple as possible. I am still anchored to the closet, but I have some more slack to work with now. Only thing is, it takes a lot out of me. It's like a game of tug-of-war. I go beyond the closet, but it's like someone is trying to pull me back, and the force is stronger the further and longer I stray." He sounded a little tired as he spoke, but he sounded more than content. "I have to go back eventually to rest and recharge before I can possibly wander out again."

He didn't sound too happy about that, not that I blamed him. As I saw it, he went from solitary confinement to normal jail with allotted recess. It was rather sad the more I thought about it, and I couldn't help but feel sadness bubble up in my chest the more I looked at his broken expression. Even if he tried to smile at me, I could see the shattered look in his grey eyes.

"Are you close to figuring out how to fully free yourself? What's wrong with the gate anyways that caused you to be trapped?" We've never touched the topic throughout this whole time, mainly because there was never really a good time to bring the elephant into the room.

Remaining quiet, Valphan averted his gaze from me to the closet. Slowly, his arms tightened around me, more so in a protective manner than one of longing. "No." He bit out dryly after an awkward silence, turning my concern for him stale.

Deciding to bite the bullet, I looked up at him with determination. "Val—mhmphf!" Only to have it all melt when his lips sealed over mine and stole my words from my tongue.

"Let me enjoy this moment, please. You are a bundle of happiness in my arms, and I want to soak it all up before I have to go back later." I hated how he was deflecting everything, but I couldn't bring myself to fight him the moment his pleading eyes shattered my walls, causing me to give in.

Pocketing the conversation for later, I gave him a reluctant smile and nodded before wrapping my arms around his neck. "Thank you for last night." Was I fond of being edged to Hell? No, not particularly, but I was more than grateful for the mind-blowing orgasms he ravaged my body with.

Although, speaking of orgasms.

"Wait, you never came last night." It didn't occur in my haze last night, but in my clarity now, I could clearly recall the lack of pleasure on his end. He finished me, then put me in bed after cleaning me up as best as possible with whatever washcloths he could grab from the bathroom using his shadows.

He held me all night from the closet with his shadows like every night. Every part of my mushy body was loved by his shadow's tender touch, and I clearly remember the food being shoved into my mouth along with some water. Damn jerk wouldn't let me pass out in peace until I got some substance in me, which I appreciated now after the fact.

Valphan's deep chuckle caused me to look at him with a furrowed face because I expected some dirty push from him for me to return the favor, not the sweetness that came. "All that matters is your pleasure, my little blessing. Taking advantage of you while you were in such a state would have been more than low for me when you made your wishes clear before we started." It should be illegal for Valphan to be this charming. "Besides, I have my own hand to relieve myself." He added with a chuckle.

Whining softly, I pouted up at him as a wave of disappointment washed over me. Shame was quick to follow as I dwelled on the lustful want festering in my brain and spreading down to my hardening nipples and aching nether regions. I had to turn my face away from him to hide it all, not wanting to admit the words rolling around on my tongue to him.

A jolt of pleasure zapped its way down my body from him, curling a finger under my chin and tilting my gaze up to him again. "Cupcake, what's wrong now? Please don't be upset by the fact I didn't take you. You really wouldn't have been happy with me if I had taken advantage of you." Damn asshole took my reaction all wrong, but damn him for being so sweet and caring about it.

Swallowing the lump in my throat, I shook my head softly. "That's not why I'm upset." God, did I really have to do this? I'd never be able to live it down if I had to admit my dirty desire to him. Hell, I don't think he'd let me live it down if I put it out there in the world.

Concern etched into every wrinkle of his scrunched-up face as he gently held my face with both hands. "What is wrong then, my little blessing? Are you hurt somewhere? Had I said something to upset you? How can I make it right?" His frantic eyes fretted my body from head to toe.

Dryly, I chuckled, "No, Fawny, no." Grabbing his face with my hands, I squished his cheeks together as I held him firm on me. "I'm not hurt or anything, and you didn't do or say anything to upset me, promise," I assured him with a smile, wiggling his face softly from side to side. "I just..." God, I could feel the heat rushing to my cheeks at the thought. "It's embarrassing..."

"Little blessing. You can ask me to streak down the street in a clown costume, and I would not find any offense in it." He joked with a chuckle and grin. "Plus, I'm a demon. I've probably already heard what you want to say."

Mumbling under my breath, I stubbornly chewed at the inside of my cheeks for a moment before reluctantly relenting. "I wanted your cock... I wanted to touch you and taste you..." Well, I should have said 'I want' instead of wanted because I still strongly desired him.

Chuckling, Valphan tightened his hold on my face and brought me within inches of his smirking lips.

"Then be a good girl and beg for it."

Chapter 12
Valphan

~1 week later~

Disappointingly, she did not beg for it at that time.

Not that I blamed her. It was new territory for her, and I was more than proud of her for admitting such a lewd want through her shyness.

"Fawn?" I still haven't gotten her to stop calling me that stupid nickname. "Fawny." Maybe if I ignored her and gave her a little silent treatment... "Fawnyyyyy."

Nope, can't do it.

Relenting with a heavy sigh, I peeped my head up from my pillow at her. "Yes, cupcake?" It was hard not to sound annoyed from being a little pent-up and irked with the nickname.

Poking her cheek with a finger, she fumbled over her words for a second before getting things out fully. "Is it possible for a man to like screw a person under him while on all fours? Like straight legs and just hunched over, not hands and knees. And, like, do that for a long while?"

Okay, it was hard not to be peeved at her cuteness. The way she tried to show me the position using her fingers and small body gestures was too amusing, paired with her awkwardness. I couldn't help but stifle a laugh as I watched her try to explain the scene she was working on, using her hands to mime her words.

I actually had to debate that one for a few seconds before I could give her a solid answer. "Well, possible, yes, but uncomfortable after a while. I imagine your legs would start cramping unless you are conditioned to it." The thought of keeping limbs straight for such a long stretch without prior conditioning sounded not so fun, and my muscles ached in protest to the thought. "I mean, even when I screwed around in my other form, I gotta bend my legs eventually or change positions," I muttered without much thought to my comment.

Gracie's eyes widened as she leaned away from me in her seat. "What?" With the way her face twisted with concern and shock, it felt like she watched me sprout a third horn out of my forehead. "I'm sorry, but your what form?" Her eyes blinked at me in disbelief as she gave me a horrified smile.

"It's nothing, it's in the past." I tried to shove the subject past us, but Gracie was not having any of it.

Scrambling out of her chair, she marched right up to the closet entrance and jabbed her finger at my face. "Nah, ah, ah, no." Pouting, she glared at me softly as she leaned her face down, settling a hand on her hip. "You don't just drop a bomb like that, then tell me to forget it, Fawny. So, spill." She demanded with firm eyes.

"Well, it's not really something I took up here with me since you humans aren't too needing of it." Now, I was deflecting in hopes of her dropping the subject matter.

The small frown from Gracie tugged my heart down with it. "Do you not like that part of you or something? You don't really sound all that happy about me poking and prodding at you." Soft regret lined her words as she pulled back from me a little.

My chest deflated with a heavy sigh as my bones creaked in protest from my upward movement to sit up. "Little blessing," I sighed, reaching out to grab her and pull her into my lap. "It's not that I don't like that part of me. It's just something that I've been so out of touch with that I don't know how to handle it."

Holding her tightly, I nuzzled my face into her neck to breathe her in. "Back in Hell, before I became a Gatekeeper, I was like any other demon of my race. We were in charge of tormenting those in the tundra, which often included chasing and hunting them down through the dense, frozen forests." Joyful memories of my various hunts throughout my lifetime caused my body to tingle excitedly. "My species, along with many others in the frozen planes, adapted a second form for the wilderness and hunts."

It was actually rather common for demonkind to adopt an alternate form to fit their environment better. I only saw a lack of an adapted form in younglings or city folk who rarely ventured beyond the walls' safety.

"I didn't really need my adapted form up on this realm because hunting in my normal form is more than sufficient." The demons and spirits up here weren't anywhere near the ones back home, so the extra effort really wasn't needed. Also, humans didn't really take too well to seeing a massive monster from their nightmares roam around their streets.

A few soft nudges against my cheek forced my head back to look at Gracie's curious and hopeful smile that lifted her eyes and made them shine. "Do you think you can show me one day?"

Cracking a soft smile, I leaned in and kissed her. "Maybe one day, when I am free. I know for a fact that I will want to run and let loose, which I can't do here without running the risk of unintentionally hurting you." I could feel the beast within me banging against its cage to be unleashed, and the moment I gave in, I'd dive head-first into a frenzy.

Letting a peaceful silence befall us, I let myself fully relax into her after pulling her down to my makeshift bed. "When I am free of this closet, can I share your bed with you? Please?" If I had it my way, I'd constantly have my arms around her, hanging off her like some clingy monkey.

Chuckling softly, my mate snuggled her face into my chest, letting me feel the movement of her lips lifting into a smile. "We'll cross that bridge when we come to it. Right now, let's take things one day at a time like how we've been."

It wasn't a rejection, so I'll gladly take the answer. Even if I wasn't fond of the whole take it slow thing, I had no choice because I was tied.

However, there was one thing... "Gracie, where are we though? What are we?"

Chapter 13
Gracie

THE DREADED QUESTION I'D been avoiding since my orgasmic night and heavenly morning with him.

Holding a tense breath, I had an inkling of hope that if I passed out, then I could avoid this conversation further. Too bad my natural instincts to breathe kicked in the moment my vision became splotchy, forcing me to let out a disgruntled huff.

I didn't pounce on him last week because I chickened out at the overwhelming feelings from my heart. Internally, I was torn. My heart knew my place with Valphan, but my rational mind held me on the safety of land. I should take the plunge, but how much would be natural with Valphan? And how much would it be because of this magical bond of destiny? I didn't want to be with him because it was deemed so. I wanted organic growth and to fall in love with my own volition. Not because my feelings were set by God!

Not that I was being an ungrateful brat so please don't smite me, big guy. And yeah, I might have grown up praying for Mister Right to come along, but come on a demon? Really? Granted, he was a charming one, and sweet, and perfect... Really, minus the demon part, he was perfect, personality-wise. And pretty sure we'd have no problems in the bedroom if that one night was any indicator.

But I couldn't be with a demon. Even if Stella and Kastoron made it work, it just didn't seem fully rational to me. I mean, at the end of the day, Valphan deserved so much more than me. He seemed like a great demon, and I was a little hermit of an introvert who spent her life on a computer as an editor and aspiring author. I only ever left the house for a makeup gig with Stella if her client didn't have someone lined up.

Clearing my head with a sigh, I zoned my attention back to Valphan, who looked down at me with broken eyes full of concern. I hated how my answer would do nothing to alleviate his anticipation. "I don't know... I wish I could give you a better answer, but I'm still a little torn." I admitted truthfully with a grimace. I wish I had a straight answer for my own sake.

Breaking into a sad smile, Valphan strokes my cheeks with the tips of his claws. "What is making you feel torn? Is it something I have done? Something I need to do? Tell me what it is that you need of me." God, I hated how eager he always was whenever it came to me. It made me feel worse about passively rejecting him and keeping him in the grey zone.

Yes, it was beyond sweet of him to cater to me, to ensure my happiness and safety above even his own needs and wants, but by God, it made my inner turmoil worse.

"It's not you." Now, I was sure I sounded like a dumb movie. "It's me."

Grasping his wrist, I brought his hand down to my stomach to play with his fingers. "You are sweet, charming, a gentleman, just perfect, really, but I'm just torn because I want to feel for you naturally. I don't want any kind of sway from this soulmate bond of ours, to love you mindless because I was destined to." The understanding frown on Valphan's face was a punch to the gut.

"But..." I wanted to turn his head away when I saw how his eyes lit up, making whatever guilt I had churn in the pits of my stomach. "Maybe things will change with time. I mean, you are growing on me quite a bit and fast, my little Fawn." I teased with a dry chuckle.

At the sound of his nickname, Valphan rolled his eyes and groaned. "Why do you keep calling me that and the other variations of it? It's the most weird nickname ever."

Giggling sheepishly, I let go of his hand to make a horn with my two index fingers at the side of my head. "Because you remind me of a baby deer with how your short horns kinda go backward and look like deer ears, and the golden color of your hair looks like their coats, too." My fingers moved with my words, mimicking his brushed-back horns. "And your hair reminds me of a fawn coat on animals."

His white-gray skin and the golden brownish hair didn't help ease my image of him being an animal. If he didn't look so demon-like and much cuter, he could look like a golden retriever—in my humble opinion.

Oh! Actually...

Rolling away from him, I reached around him to pull the faux fur blanket over him with a snicker. "And the fact you love to bundle yourself up in this and curl up into a cute ball really reminds me of Goldie, who has a fawn-ish coat."

Playfully narrowing his eyes at me, Valphan huffed and pulled me under the blanket with him. "I don't know whether to be offended that you compared me to your mutt again along with a weak little baby deer or happy and grateful for putting such thought and attention to me." He grumbled with a roll of his eyes.

Tightening his arms around me, he pressed my frontside flushed against his. An arm around my waist and lower back to keep me anchored, he ran the other through my pink locks. "Why do you color your hair? Why pink?" He asked while carefully observing my hair slipping between his fingers.

"I like pink." That was the main reason. "Being a brown-haired Asian is boring, and pink is fun, cute, and happy." Taking my hair from him, I giggled and tickled his nose with the tips of my hair. "Also, it's a way to stick it to my parents because they want me to be normal and boring."

"Speaking of your parents, what the fuck were they thinking naming you Prudence?" I couldn't help but laugh a little at how he sounded offended for me about my name.

Letting my laughter die out to a dry chuckle, I picked at the splint ends of my strands while speaking, "They're hardcore religious people, like read, eat, and drink the bible for breakfast, lunch, and dinner hardcore. They wanted me to basically be the demure housewife and pop out kids and kiss my husband's feet for letting me breathe. They wanted me on the 'right' path and thought if they gave me the right namesake or whatever, then I'd stick to it."

Sighing heavily, I dropped my hands back to his, "Only thing it brought me was a lot of bullying growing up, and I guess, in a way, I was shown a life I definitely *didn't* want for my future." Maybe if I had been home-schooled and shut inside for the majority of my life, then I'd live the life my parents wanted so desperately for me.

Fortunately, I suffered the outside life that opened my eyes the older I got. Sure, my life could be a lot more stable than it is now, but I've nothing to complain about. I had my own place, didn't have to put up with my parents—again—had jobs I thoroughly enjoyed, and I had Valphan—life was perfect in hindsight. Most importantly, I was content. Yes, even with a demon living in my closet and being an indoor girl, I was very content.

"They're probably not gonna like me very much then when they meet me." The lightheartedness in his voice meant he was joking—thank God.

Laughing softly, I tilted my head up at him, reached up, and pinched his cheek. "They'd have a heart attack the moment they hear I'm dating someone who isn't of our religion. If they heard their precious daughter fell for a demon, well, pretty sure they'd explode into a pile of ashes in their spots." I threw my own joking words back at him.

Then, as my fingers lingered against his cheek, my curiosity emboldened me. Slowly, I traced my fingers up to his horn while holding back a smile. Stella told me about how sensitive Kastoron was with his horns, so I was curious to see for myself now that I had my own little demon to mess around with.

"Cupcake, don't do what you're thinking." Valphan's warning rumbled out of his chest as his body went stiff under me.

Stopping right at the base of his horn, I let my fingers linger while I looked at him with a raised eyebrow. "Why do you call me that? Cupcake? Little blessing?" A small moment of distraction won't hurt.

The uncontrolled grin, paired with how his eyes lit up like a sunny day, caused my body to explode with a wave of hot bliss and for my heart to thud away like some war drum. "Because you are my saving grace." Suffocating me with a hug, he let out a happy sound of a humming chuckle. "I'll never be able to fully show you how grateful I am, even if we are to spend eternity with each other."

Kissing the top of my head, he gave me one final squeeze before pulling back to look down at me. "For centuries, I remained trapped in a never-ending darkness in a suspended state, unable to fully sleep or wake until you came along." Tracing the edge of my face with his finger, he smiled at me tenderly. "Your voice pulled me from the void the moment I heard it. You woke me from what could have possibly been an eternity of damnation."

Shivers of arousal warmed my body until I felt myself clench around nothing when his lips descended onto mine in a languid kiss. "You brought me back to life, literally, so therefore my blessing." He whispered against my lips. "I will forever be grateful for whatever divinity brought you to me, and I will forever cherish you until I fade away to nothing when I choose to be done with life."

Then, his smile turned playful and cute. "As for cupcake," chuckling, he boops my nose, "I got the idea from your hair and light creamy complexion after you kept looking at cupcakes. The pink looks like frosting, and your light, creamy skin resembles vanilla cake."

"Okay, a little cheesy but sweet and cute," I remarked with a giggle before leaning up and kissing him softly.

Pressing my finger firmly against the base of his horn, I slowly traced the edge of it, causing Valphan's eyes to darken with his shudder. "How about you save your energy to come out later tonight?"

Intrigued, Valphan smirked in response with raised brows. "Oh? For?"

"A date."

Valphan's face lit up brighter than a damn Christmas tree with the big ass grin that spread on his face, and I couldn't help but let his contagious happiness spread to my face.

Chapter 14

Valphan

~2 weeks later~

"Cupcake, unless your character is a contortionist, this whole scene isn't too plausible without a lot of pain."

From the corner of my eyes, I watched her puff her cheeks out with a huff before stuffing her mouth full of pasta. "But it works in porn." She retorted in a grumble after swallowing her mouthful.

"Porn isn't real, pinkie." I teased with a soft laugh. "But by all means, if you want to test it out personally, I'm more than happy to act out these scenes of hers."

Wickedly grinning, I peered over the book at her while slouching on the couch. "I wouldn't be opposed to putting you into a full nelson or tying you to a tree after a chase and claiming you like a trophy." For a little virgin, the stuff she came up with for her book kind of surprised me.

You definitely won't hear a complaint from me, though. A kinky mate meant home on earth for me.

Lucifer, the thought of shoving her out into the little wooded area in her backyard on a night when the skies were clear of clouds with the moon and stars lighting the earth up and chasing her frantic body through the foliage. Fuck, a dream come true, I tell you. Such fantasies made my bones ache and creak for a change and run to get that fresh air and adrenaline rush before letting it explode.

"Fawny, you have that look again." Her wary voice carried over from the kitchen counter, where she sat eating her dinner.

"Oh?" Setting the book down in my lap, I gave my full, curious attention to her. "What look?" I was more than aware of my twisted thrill surfacing, but I wanted to see her blush and squirm a little.

Her cheeks continued to redden until I swear she looked like a cherry. "Like you're going to pounce on me and ravage me." She squeaked with a gulp.

"Because I want to." I couldn't hold back my feral grin as I eyed her hungrily. "I want to throw you onto the bed, rip your clothes off, spread those plush legs of yours apart, make my cock disappear into your precious cunt, and screw you until you're all filled with my cum." If I had no heart for my little blessing, I would have done that the moment I was freed from limbo. "I'd fuck you so crazy and stuff you so full that you'd be leaking my seed for days."

A deep, needy groan escaped me as lustful images of Gracie under me consumed my every thought and filled my body with burning desire. "Then, to let loose in my beast form and hunt you down and claim you on the fresh soil of the earth or right up against a tree after stringing you up like a meal." Maybe I should indulge myself a little, take what I wanted for once when it came to Gracie.

The soft clatter of her silverware hitting porcelain snapped me from my thoughts with a pang of concern. I thought perhaps something happened to cause such a sound, so the last thing I expected was to see Gracie's hips swaying heavily toward me with each of her taunting steps. "What else do you want to do to me?" Sweet sultry saturated her voice as she crawled onto the couch and into my lap, straddling it.

Reaching out, she boldly grabbed my horns and pulled my gasping face right up to her smirking lips, leaving barely a hair between us. "Have you been getting some ideas from helping me edit my books? Thinking about us in such positions instead of whatever character I made for my stories?"

Gripping her hips tightly, I sucked in a shaky breath. "Gracie, don't tease me tonight unless you intend on doing something about my problem or will let me use your lovely body for relief." If it were any other night, then I'd let her have some fun, but I was too pent up tonight.

Teasing her lips across mine with a sultry giggle, she traces the length of my horn with the tips of her fingers as her hips press down against mine. "I won't let you chase me through the woods tonight, not after a big ass bowl of pasta, but if you can get me in the mood, then I'll let you have your pie and eat it."

Burying my face into her neck with a groan, I held my urges back as I dug my claws into her plush behind. "Prudence Grace, I only have so much control, and when you say things like that, it does things to me." I strained out through gritted teeth. "I want you so bad, but I know the moment I get you naked under me—fuck!"

I wanted to shred her clothes off this very instant and take her on the couch, pounding into her until she screamed for mercy. But I can't, not now, at least. All of that would be too much for her virgin body to take right out of the gate.

"Valphan," her sweet voice dragged my desire for her out to the surface. "Valphan, look at me." How could I deny her demand when it was so alluring?

Relenting with a groan, I craned my head back to look at her with half-hooded eyes. "My little blessing, please." I silently begged for mercy as I let myself melt under her warm gaze.

"I trust you."

Three simple words.

Three simple but magical words.

And it was all it took to erode all my inhibitions.

"I hope you really mean it and know the implications of placing such trust in me." Though eternally grateful, I wanted her to be sure. "Hearing those three words from you means that you are giving me all of you. Your mind, body, and soul are being trusted to me. For me to cherish and ruin as I see fit, to own and love."

My last wispy thread of control completely disappeared with her assertive words. "Valphan, I am all yours. I might not be experienced, but I trust you to care for me. Do whatever you want to me, push me down to the endless depths of the oceans and pull me back to the surface, take me to Hell and back." Cupping my face tenderly, she smiled proudly. "I know I am safe with you, so I trust you not to harm me."

Groaning needily, I kissed her deeply with a racing heart as pure bliss and lust consumed every fiber of my being. "Sweet Lilith, I didn't think falling deeper for you was possible, but fuck..." I growled against her lips before summoning some shadow tendrils to wrap themselves around our bodies.

Impatiently, I slid my hands down her body to her backside, gripping her big ass firmly to support her as I stood and took us to her room. "Are you absolutely sure? I can be gentle, and I will be with you tonight as much as possible, but I can't make any promises as the night drags on." It would be hard not to pound away at her later when I'd enter her fully.

The mere thought of her tight walls choking my thick member already made me want to rip a hole in her bottoms and fuck her right here in the hallway. It would be like walking through Heaven later when the time came for me to take her virginity (not fun because I'm a demon). I was ready to endure the torture of keeping myself back for as long as possible for her sake later, though. I wanted the moment to be special for Gracie, but not because it was her first time ever. No. This moment *needed* to be special for her because it would be her first time with me and the start of something new for both of us.

Tonight would be the start of our new lives together.

We may have been living like a married couple as of late, especially after we got a routine going between us, but there was a deeper aspect to it all that had been missing. Tonight, everything would fall into place with each other for us.

Looking up at me with a happy and resolute smile, Gracie stroked the length of my jaw up to my horn. "I am all yours to do away with as you please, Valphan. Whether you fuck me like you hate me or take things slow and languid, I will be eternally grateful for it and find pleasure in it all." Leaning up, she kissed me deeply with a soft moan.

Hopefully, I don't make her regret all of it later when I inevitably lose what little control I had a slipping grasp on.

It didn't take long for me to reach the bedroom with the eager strides I took. Then, as tempting as it was to literally throw her onto the bed and ravage her, I kept myself in check enough to set her down like the precious princess she was.

The intention to slowly strip her flew out the window the moment I ran my hands up her body and groped a feel of her small breasts. With her flimsy shirt fisted tightly, I tore it away in a forceful pull, making her gasp and protest by flailing her fists against my chest. As if that would stop me from tearing the rest of her clothes away with my impatience ramping up.

"Valphan! You better be prepared to give me a whole new closet if you keep destroying my clothes like this!" She huffed with a pouty glare. "Seriously, between your little late-night pleasurings of me and your bed, I've got little to no clothes left."

With a cheeky grin, I gripped the waistband of her shorts and panties, ripping them away in another hard movement. "You wear the same outfits every damn day. I only use and ruin the ones you obviously don't need." I remarked with a roll of my eyes before settling myself between her legs and spreading them with a hungry grin on my face.

"Excuse you, I needed those dresses and the blouses." She argued with a little kick and shove to my chest with her foot.

Grumbling under my breath, I ran my hands down her legs, lingering against her inner thighs to rub the softness with my rough hands. "No, you don't. You bought those gaudy little outfits for dates, which you don't ever need in your life now that you have me."

To be fair, she had a right to be upset about how I destroyed her property because I was jealous and a little petty, but if she had nothing nice to wear, she couldn't go out, meaning she'd spend more time around me. As for my nesting tendencies with her things, that was because I needed to pass my boredom. Also, being surrounded by her scent comforted me, and feeling her soft clothes against my body gave me the illusion that she was physically there with me.

"W-what if they were for you?" She retorted weakly with an averted gaze.

Unable to help myself, I laughed a little at her attempt to argue back. "Cupcake, you can't fool a demon." I mused with my dying chuckle.

Teasingly, I parted her folds with slow strokes until her swollen clit was exposed to me. "I can't wait til I'm free to wake up between your legs." Frustration bubbled in my chest at the fact of my continuing imprisonment, but I quickly shoved it away because that was a problem for a different time.

"Fuck you to sleep at night, hold you throughout, then wake up to breakfast in bed." I teased with a cheeky grin before hooking my arms around her hips as I lowered myself down to her irresistible cunt. "Hope you're ready to go crazy from coming."

Ignoring her protest, I latched my starving mouth onto her addictive sex, sucking and licking at her like a juicy forbidden fruit. No inch of her was left untouched by my lavishing tongue that lapped at her like a thirsty hound. Forcing her legs to remain wide open with my big head and horns, I moved my head from side to side to get as much of her into my mouth as possible while stimulating her, causing her sweet moans to hike up in pitch and volume.

"Valphan! Too much!" She squealed with a loud moan as her jerking hips tried to buck away from me during the aftershocks of her orgasm.

Her frantic hands threw themselves into my hair and horns, gripping wildly at them as I pressed into her more to drive her up the wall with maddening pleasure. I didn't begin to let up until her cunt spasmed against my mouth and tongue, and her juices squirted out of her with every jerk of her tense body.

Now, I would have stopped sooner rather than later if it weren't for her tugging at my horns to fuck my face. Well, she bucked her hips at me a few times before trying to pull away because of the stimulation. It was sweet to see the struggle for more while her body was overstimulated, to see the fight in her lustful eyes.

Tightening my grip on her hips, I shoved her overly sensitive body over the edge once more, making her shake the air with her scream of rapture when I pulled another orgasm from her shaking body.

My chest rumbled with a chuckle as I pulled my dripping face away, grinning madly down at her as I licked every bit of her off my face with my long tongue. "Fucking delicious." I wanted to sandwich my head between her pillowy thighs and lick at her like ice cream for the rest of the night.

Well, maybe not tonight because the need to get myself balls-deep in her overrode my want.

But first...

"Open up."

Chapter 15

Gracie

"HUH?"

Did he say something?

Actually... Is any of this real?

My body fucking ached but in a good way. But why? And why was I crying? My cheeks were wet, but I didn't...

"Gracie, cupcake, open up." Then there was that sweet voice, so rich and smooth, but it had a wild edge to it, like a wound-up animal ready to pounce. "Cupcake, be my good girl and open that pretty little mouth of yours for me."

I felt my body obey the voice as if I were in a trance. My mouth eagerly fell open, ready to take in whatever was coming while I struggled to pull myself out of my daze. It was a struggle until panic jerked my body like I had been thrown into the Arctic waters.

Panicking and going on instinct, my hands tightened into fists and flew at the mass in front of me as burning-hot tears welled up in my eyes and scorched their way down my cheeks. Violently, my body jerked with my gags as I choked on something big that kept forcing its way in and out of my throat.

Whatever was above me rumbled under my struggling hands. "Fuck, you look lovely crying and choking on my cock right now, cupcake." Cupcake?

His cupcake... Right... Bed and Valphan. Oh fuck, we're gonna fuck.

Snapping out of it fully, I blinked my tears away to clear my vision while my body continued to struggle against the foreign object in my mouth and throat. Well, the object wasn't *foreign* per se; I'd gotten used to seeing Valphan's junk at this point in time with how often he jerked off to me from the closet at night. Still, I've never gotten this close to it.

Hell, how did he even fit the thing inside of my mouth without breaking my jaw? I mean, I knew I had a big mouth at times, but even wide open, I'd barely be able to take most of his tip in if I dared try. So, how the fuck was I taking nearly all of it right now? Unless I was dead, which I doubted because I very much felt alive with how hot my body burned with desire for my demon lover right now.

"Relax and breathe through your nose." He instructed me while slowing his thrusts.

Yeah, as if that were simple to do. He wasn't the one choking on a demon dick currently!

I tried my best to do as he said, but I found myself coughing and gagging with each and every attempt. Although, I don't think any of it deterred him with how he kept fucking my face like there was no tomorrow. If anything, I think my struggles spurred him on further because he went harder and faster at me.

Then, just as I was adjusting, he abruptly pulled out, leaving me gasping and coughing for air. A harsh grip and jerk of my face forced my attention to Valphan. "Eyes on me, Gracie. I'm the only man you are ever allowed to lay eyes on from here on out. The only being you are allowed to look up to because I am your god now." His feral grin sent a shudder of arousal down my body, making my sensitive nipples tighten against his thighs while my aching pussy wept to be stuffed.

A sharp gasp gripped my throat as I flinched at the sudden splatter of heat streaking across my face and chest. Sputtering in shock, all I could do was stare completely dumbfounded at Valphan as he jerked off his spurting cock, emptying a load of cum onto my face. A low chuckle caused my eyes to snap back up to his cheeky face. "This should be the only outfit you ever wear." He mused while swiping his thumb across my cheek and forcing it into my mouth. "My cum, and nothing else."

By some unknown instinct, I found myself wrapping my lips around his thumb to suck and lick the tangy, salty essence of him off his finger. Not gonna lie, it tasted strong, but for some reason, that didn't turn me off like how it would with the previous men I'd sucked off in the past. I found myself enjoying Valphan's cum, needily sucking and licking his thumb completely clean and then some in hopes of catching a stray taste.

When he withdrew his thumb, I let out a whiny whimper as I tried to follow with my head, only to have him hold me firm and shove his cock back into my mouth. As much as I wanted to protest, any fight I had washed away the moment his taste filled my mouth again. Eagerly, I sucked and licked at his throbbing tip, hoping to squeeze out a drop or two of his precious cum.

"Fuck, if I knew you were such a cock hungry slut then I would have done this a lot sooner." He groaned with a shudder, his hand releasing my face to grip the top of my head. "You're going to be my good little cum dumping slut, aren't you?"

God, that was so degrading, and I should slap him across the face after biting his dick for saying that to me. But fuck me, it turned me on so much. I'd gladly let myself be reduced to nothing but a needy whore for Valphan and only him. Something about him tugged at my depraved desires and breathed life into my dark heart.

Pulling off his cock, I looked up at him with my lust-dazed eyes as I kissed and licked along his textured cock. "Yes, I wanna be your cum dump. I want you to make me your slut tonight and every night." I spoke hastily against his cock while I loved it with sloppy and needy kisses.

Leaning down, Valphan kissed me heavily and sloppily, shoving his tongue deep into my mouth. Soft creaks from the bed giving under his weight interrupted the air around us as he moved his body back down between my legs.

Breaking the kiss, he rested his forehead against me while panting hotly. "I'm going to keep these sheets forever in storage to keep a memory of this night for eternity."

He chuckled against my lips before kissing me softly and intertwining his fingers with mine.

Pining my hands down by my head, he nudged my legs wider apart to settle his hips against my inner thighs. With a few teasing bucks of his hips, he rubbed the full length of his cock against my slit, slickening himself up with my juices.

Then, I swear, his cock grew bigger. Well, correction: his cock grew to his normal size. I think. "W-wait, can you change your dick?" I didn't mean to ask that question right now and possibly ruin the moment, but I had no control over my mouth.

Chuckling softly, he angled his hips to prod at my virgin entrance with his massive tip. "Yes, but I prefer to keep myself natural because I've nothing to be ashamed of with it. I only shrunk myself to feel your sweet mouth and lips around me." He replied before pressing into me, causing me to wince with a sharp gasp. "I've no need to make myself bigger."

Through my shallow breaths, I could hear Valphan mutter something under his breath before a rush of heat made me shudder. "Don't ever make yourself bigger, you're already so fucking huge." I groaned through the buzz of my system. "What did you just do?" I felt so heated with lust that I swear I might go crazy.

Kissing me softly a few times, he teased my entrance with his tip while he replied, "A protection spell so you can take me and to keep you from getting pregnant, and something to ease your nerves."

Even though his tip hurt like a bitch, I wanted more to quell this growing inferno in me. "Fucking asshole, my body is on fire!" I strained through gritted teeth as I fought the urge to hump at him like a dog in heat.

Then, with a sheepish chuckle, Valphan looked at me with an apologetic smile before plunging himself balls-deep with a harsh thrust. Even though I was horny as hell, no way was I prepared for the sheer pain that felt like someone forced me to do a split on a pike.

My mouth hung open in a silent scream. Tears rushed down my face like waterfalls as I dug my nails into the back of Valphan's hands with my death grip.

Burying his face into my neck, he hissed something in another language before pulling back with a deep breath. "Of fuck!" Valphan strained out a groan. "You're going to make me embarrass myself if you keep squeezing me like that." His breaths came out strangled and heavy as his hips jerked against me in a struggle.

"You're going to break me if you move." I struggled through gasping breaths, digging my hips into the bed in an attempt to pull myself away from the pain of his cock. "You're stretching me so much, filling me so much, and those damn bumps of yours. I can feel each and every one of them." It hurt to clench around him to get a better feel of him, but my greedy body kept wanting more despite my brain telling it to stop for a moment.

"Breathe, sweetheart, you'll pass out if you keep gasping and not letting it out." Valphan let out a strangled breath of his own as he ground his hips against me, causing every inch of his cock to rub against my spasming walls. "You need to breathe and relax before you make me come." His hips came to a stop with a firm press, and he gripped my hands in return as his eyes squinted shut with his furrowed brows.

"I-isn't that... Isn't that the whole point of fucking me? To dump your load in me and be done?" Wasn't that the point of sex, period? Fuck to get the fun, then leave?

Well, besides the point of sex being used as a means of procreating, wasn't it just a fun way to release?

I didn't like the thought of it one bit, Valphan and I falling into some comfortable situationship with each other. Yes, I wanted him to fuck me, but I wanted more than sex from him.

Over the past weeks, I'd grown so used to our weird routine of him waking me with breakfast, pampering me in the bath or shower after a long day of work, and even while I worked, he'd be holding me or getting the knots out of my shoulders and neck. Then, as the day went on, he'd do all the house chores while I worked after he sensed my need for space. Honestly, I don't think I've had to do a single load of laundry or wash a plate since he took over the house chores.

However, the routine brought a newfound fondness for Valphan. The thought of one day losing what we've created or not being together in any way broke my heart into pieces. I didn't want to admit it because I was too stubborn and afraid of commitment.

The more I lingered on my reservations, the more the air around us instantly changed from hot and heavy to awkward and draggy.

Valphan's face softened with worry as he opened his eyes again. Softly, he nudged my cheek with his nose. "Hey, do you need me to stop?" He didn't even wait for me to answer before slowly peeling his hip away, making me wince at the emptying feeling.

I don't know what came over me, but my legs coiled around his waist like a python striking its prey. Trapping him, I forced us back together fully with a pained grunt. "No! Don't stop... Please." Afraid he'd pry himself away, I dug my nails more into him while my legs tightened around his waist.

"Gracie." His worried eyes frantically searched my face as his body stiffened against me. "If you've changed your mind, that's okay. Don't force yourself into anything, even if we are in the middle of it." Pressing his forehead against mine, he gently kissed my lips. "I want this moment to be memorable in a happy way, not in a horrible way where you get filled with regret and hatred every time you think back to this night."

Unable to help it, I pulled my lips into a natural smile at his sweet words. "Valphan, I'm not regretting anything." Pausing for a second, I swallowed my pride and struggled for a moment to get out my feelings. "I'm terrified of what will happen after tonight... And I'm terrified of how this is making me realize how much I love you."

Breaking out in an incredible smile, Valphan released my hands to embrace me and trapped my head in a soul-sucking kiss. "I'm definitely not stopping after you say something like that." With renewed energy, he started to buck his hips at me in short and slow thrusts. "If this makes you love me more, then I'm fucking you until you feel nothing but utter devotion toward me."

Grinning madly, he pried my legs off him to pin them against the bed, nearly folding me like some pretzel. "Let's see how much I can make you love me." The wild glint in his eyes made mine widen as my mouth opened in a loud moan from his sudden thrust.

With some shadow hands holding my legs open and down to the bed, he grabbed my hands again before thrusting in and out of me with no mercy. The lewd sounds of our bodies slapping violently against each other echoed throughout the rooms with Valphan's animalistic groans and my screams of pleasure. I couldn't control anything that came out of my mouth in response to his monstrous cock forcing my cunt to mold itself to him. Every little movement caused his raised bumps to rub against my sensitive walls as his girth would part me. Then his tip, fuck his hard tip hit so deep and right that my eyes rolled with each thrust.

Bunching my wrists up in one hand, he uses his freed one to grab my neck and squeeze at it before exaggerating his thrusts. "How." Thrust. "Much." Thrust. "Do." Thrust. "You." Thrust. "Love." Thrust. "Me." Thrust. "Now!?"

His words barely made it through the fog of pleasure in my mind as I struggled to keep my rolling eyes on Valphan. Every hard thrust from him jarred my body, despite his grip on me, making me feel like a bobblehead doll the further into insanity he fucked me.

I barely managed to whimper my words through my jagged moans and grunts. "A lot. Love you. Much. So much." It came out as full sentences in my mind, but my tongue refused to work with me.

"Aww, would you look at that." Valphan mocked me with a wicked grin as he shook my face back and forth. "My little blessing is at a loss for words for once. Guess I fucked my slutty little mate too good and stupid."

Did he slacken his thrusts? No, no, he did not. In fact, the damn asshole went harder and faster at me until I full-on screamed and saw stars from orgasming. "My God." I sobbed through the aftershock of my orgasm. "Valphan!"

That only spurred him on more. His smug laughter filled the air as he slammed into me with such a bruising force. "That's fucking right! I'm your God!" He sounded like he enjoyed that a tad too much. "The big man can take it up with me later, but the only divine being you're allowed to get on your knees and worship is me. You got that, slut?"

A slew of stringless 'yeses' sputtered from me uncontrollably as I was caught in the throes of pleasure. "Valphan...

Please... Fill me, please... Fill me with your cum. Need you so bad." The mere thought of having his hot seed fill my womb and remain once he pulled his cock back made my body tremble with a small orgasm, causing me to clench around him in an attempt to coax him.

"Fucking fiery pits of home, I can't wait to fucking hunt you down and claim you fully." He snarled with a deep growl as he sped up his thrusts. "Right after our soul binding, when you're still in your pretty little dress. Just chase you down through the forest, hold you down, and fuck your brains out before biting and knotting you."

With a groan, his hips jerked out of rhythm until he buried himself fully in me. "Fuck, Gracie, sweetie, fucking love you so much." His words washed over my face hotly before his lips devoured mine in a passionate kiss, one I barely managed to return because I was blanking out from the searing pleasure of my orgasm.

"It's okay, my blessing, I got you." His words faded into the background, sounding like a whisper. "Let yourself go, it's okay."

"I love you so much, Valphan." I barely managed to squeak out before I felt my hold on reality slip.

The last thing I remembered was the feeling of something warm pressing against my temple. "I will forever be grateful for your love and spend forever loving you back, my little blessing." There were some other words, but I couldn't make it out.

I didn't care. All I ever needed in life was within my grasp.

I had my Valphan, my happiness and peace in life.

Chapter 16

Valphan

~1 month later~

"Please?"

I sighed for the umpteenth time at my mate's insistent pleading. Rubbing my temples with a groan, I tightly bundled the blanket around myself. "Cupcake, I'm not saying no for the hell of it." And I've told her the reason already a few times. "It's too dangerous."

"Fawny." Gracie sighed with a pout as she leaned back in her desk chair. "You keep telling me about how much you're going to eat me up in your other form, tell me all the fun, get my hopes up, then refuse to even show me." She grumbled flatly with a stern glare.

Okay, that punched me in the gut with guilt because I did sweet talk the ever-living heck out of her during our late-night rumps about how crazy sex would be in my other form. To be fair, I shouldn't even be teasing her with the whole notion.

As much as I wanted to do all of it, it seemed more and more like something impossible. After studying the gate during my moments of boredom... I...

"Please, can we drop this subject again?" The subject became rather sore for me as the facts sunk into my bones.

Sighing heavily, I sat up from my spot in the closet with an apologetic smile. "One day." Maybe... Never...

"Alright... But, how far have you gotten with figuring out how to fix the gate to free yourself?" Her question made me wince involuntarily because the subject was tied to the previous.

The only problem was that she didn't know of the connection because I'd been deceiving her regarding it. It wasn't because I wanted to lie to her, though. I didn't know how to break it all to her.

This relationship of ours was still so new, to her at least. A month was fast by human standards, and even though she'd been adjusting well to me as a lover, dropping that kind of bomb on her was a sure way to lose her. Mate bond or not, I didn't want to risk anything when it came to my little blessing.

"Well, unless you're prepared to sacrifice a hundred human souls, there's no permanent escape for me." I lied smoothly through my smile with an aching heart.

Rolling her eyes, Gracie gave me a chuckle that turned dry. "Seriously, Fawny, have you figured out a way?" She asked through a forced smile.

Sighing heavily, I ran a hand through my hair. "It might not be a hundred souls... But I do need souls... So... Until I can figure out another way, this is how things will be for the foreseeable future." It wasn't a full lie, so the guilt didn't burn at my damned soul so badly.

Though, I couldn't help but laugh at myself internally at the irony of feeling guilty about lying. I mean, think about it: a demon feeling bad about lying. Yeah, fucking ironic.

"How did the gate even get messed up like that? I mean, if you're in charge of it, then what happened?" Gracie asked with a soft frown as she slid out of her chair to crawl over to me and snuggle with me.

"Gracie, you'll fall asleep on the ground again." I worried with a frown of my own. "You have a soft bed that won't fuck up your back."

Without missing a beat, she retorted, "But my bed doesn't have you, and you always beat everything in terms of comfort." Sleeping on the closet ground with me was a bad habit she'd formed throughout the past weeks ever since we started having sex more and more.

Sighing, I held her tightly against me and kissed the top of her head. I didn't know what to say for once in my life because the guilt from before swallowed me up like a void. There was a solution, but I didn't want to take it. Also, I refused to let her know about the full truth.

"But, back to before about the gate and everything... I mean, we've never really talked much about it, but I'm bored, and I have bad writer's block, so let's talk." Her finger prodded at my chest while her words pried at my mind, her sweet voice doing nothing to sway the temptation.

So, relenting with a sigh, I laid down with her atop me. "I should really try to convince you to get some more work done, but you're only going to get cranky with me if I do." I mused with a chuckle, rubbing the full length of her back with my hand.

Taking a moment of silence to collect my thoughts, I stared up at the ceiling momentarily before looking down at her round eyes peering up at me. "I came here to earth with Aesophedus and the other shadow princes to help govern over the humans with the angels God sent down. Between all of us, we're in charge of ensuring spirits go to their respective places, capturing escapees, culling the bad from humanity, and guarding over the humans."

Mindlessly twirling a lock of her hair between my fingers, I continued. "My job as a gatekeeper is to lure lost spirits to carry them to the afterlife, where they'll be judged. I also had to make sure no one or thing came back out from the other side, and if they did, I had to hunt them down."

I didn't know how deep or much I had to spill to Gracie, so I skipped to the important part she probably wanted to hear. "Long story short, some humans weren't so happy with me guiding their loved ones to the other side and not allowing them access or bringing people back to the land of the living. So, when I was out hunting one night, they fucked with my gate and were successful with it."

That dreaded night flashed through my mind like a horror movie on repeat as I recounted it for my mate. "They wanted to bring back their loved ones from the other side, and if I hadn't stopped them, then it would have been Hell on Earth. I didn't fix the gate fully, only managed to modify it enough to prevent them from entering Earth." Unintentionally, I gripped the back of her shirt out of irritation. "But in doing so, I created a barrier, where if anyone entered, they couldn't pass back unless they had certain authorities like me."

Taking a deep breath, I simmered myself. "Unfortunately, while I was doing damage control and forcing the spirits and demons back to the afterlife, the humans jumped me. The witches and warlocks managed to split my soul and body and trap me on the other side. Then they modified the gate to what it is before taking the keystone away."

Breathing in Gracie's soothing scent, I let my nerves calm. "I became trapped in an endless sleep after a while until you came along, where I woke but couldn't form my physical body until Levianth replaced that keystone." Only problem now was my soul, rather the two parts of it—the thing I refused to tell Gracie about out of fear. "In order to be fully free, the gate does need a sacrifice of a soul. Usually, that wouldn't be a problem because gateways like these are created to attract spirits, but this one was modified by the humans to deter. And I'm not exactly keen on fixing that quite yet and turning our home into a hotbed of paranormal activity while I am not at full strength or freedom to operate."

Brushing her hair out of her face, I painted her cheek with the tip of my finger while smiling at her sadly. "The last thing I want is for you to get hurt because I can't get to you in time or because of my restriction to the closet." That wasn't a lie either because it was too risky for both of us.

I was nowhere near my full strength and capabilities, so if spirits and demons stormed this place right now, I'd be fucked—not the fun kind of fucked.

Pinching the corner of her frowning lips, I pulled it into an awkward smile. "Cupcake, don't be sad. We'll figure it all out eventually." For the sake of my sanity, I needed to figure it out. I didn't want Gracie to be stuck with the label of being married to the demon stuck in a damn closet.

Hopefully, a change of subject would help. "Now, cheer up and tell me more about how far you've gotten with your story. Are you almost done?"

Forcing a smile on her face, she sighed softly with a nod of her head. "Yeah, almost done with the final touches... Just nervous about sending out the ARCs and release day." She worried her bottom lip between her teeth with a furrowed face until I squished her cheeks together with my big hand.

Grinning cheekily, I reached down and grabbed at her shorts. "You know what will help those nerves?" I asked in a suggestive tone, wiggling my eyebrows knowingly.

Laughing and rolling her eyes, Gracie slapped my chest. "Fawny, you literally screwed and stuffed me after dinner." She remarked while bucking her hips away from my hand.

Not letting her escape, I gripped her big ass and pinned her against my abdomen. "Did I say I was going to fuck you?" I wouldn't oppose the idea, but I knew she was at her limit tonight regarding sex with her demon mate.

Suddenly, the sounds of clothes ripping clawed the air. "You need to relax to sleep." I teased her wet opening with the tips of my fingers, lazily dragging them along the length of her cunt and circling her clit. "So wet," I remarked with a slow kiss. "You need to be mopped up."

Throwing her shredded bottoms and panties aside, I hoisted her up to my face. "Sit on my face," I commanded with a needy growl, my nostrils flaring at her intoxicating scent mixed with mine.

Staring down at me with wide eyes and mouth agape, she hovered over me. "Y-you can't be serious. I'm still full of your—ah!" Her body jarred forward with the forceful shove at her hips. "Valphan!"

"A real man, especially a demon, doesn't care about that shit." Grabbing her hips, I forcefully lowered her until she was less than an inch from my hungry mouth. "So, shut the fuck up and sit on my face so I can eat you out until your legs won't stop shaking."

Of course, my sweet little mate, being how she was, didn't listen. Yes, she lowered herself onto my face, but it wasn't what I wanted. So, I pulled my hand back and snapped it against her ass cheek, making her flinch and yelp. Her body jerked away from me, probably out of instinct, but I didn't let her.

Wrapping my arms around her waist, I held her tightly against my face. "I told you to fucking sit on my face," I remarked with a soft glare up at her as I gave her twitching cunt some teasing licks.

"I am." She whimpered in response, grinding her hips down against me.

Growling softly, I gave her ass another harsh slap that caused another yelp. "That's not how you fucking sit." Jerking her hips, I looked at her with dark eyes. "When I tell you to sit on my face, I want you to *sit* on it like a fucking chair."

Gracie's eyes widened slightly as her bottom lip became tucked between her teeth. "But... I'll squish you." She squeaked out with reddening cheeks.

Unable to help myself, I laughed softly at her sweetness. "Little blessing, if I die because I suffocated on your delicious cunt then that's a happy death." I joked with a hearty laugh. "Not like that would happen," I assured her with a firm smile before urging her with a nudge. "So, sit on my fucking face."

"Yes, sir." Gulping, Gracie slowly lowered herself fully onto me with a shaky breath. Hesitating, she stared down at me with wary eyes for a good moment before I felt her full weight blanket the lower half of my face.

Squishing her thighs tightly around my face, I let out a deep, blissful groan as I let the taste of our mixed juices flow into my mouth and bathe my tongue. Slithering my tongue around expertly, I licked every inch of her inside and out while my hands roamed around her curvy body to worship it with affection.

Holding her firmly against me with some shadow tendrils, I pressed my tongue firmly against her swollen clit and hummed softly to send vibrations against it. The sounds of her melodic moans filled my ears as my chest swelled with pride at the feeling of her hips grinding against my face for more.

The ferocity with which I ate her out intensified the moment her soft hands came down on my horns and pulled at them as if she were some bull rider. "Valphan, too much." Her trembling body squealed from above as her soft thighs clamped my head.

A few more swipes of my tongue along her clit and some thrusts into her tight channel caused the floodgates to bust open. Her loud moans filled my ears while her juices filled my mouth at a rate where I almost couldn't keep up. It probably didn't help that I kept on overstimulating her, forcing her to orgasm over and over when I already shoved her over the edge and into deep waters.

I couldn't help myself though. My little mate tasted too damn amazing and addicting. Even as I lapped up every single drop of her precious juices, the need for more urged my tongue forward to squeeze more out of her. I wanted to spend forever between her legs, eat her out until she would constantly have a fucked out face full of pure bliss.

The feeling of something wet hitting my face pulled me out of my lustful daze to look up at Gracie, who had tears streaming down her face while her mouth hung open. "Valphan, I can't stop coming." She sobbed in a voice saturated with sweet suffering.

Deciding to take some mercy on my mate, I pulled three more orgasms from her before slowing to a stop and releasing her from me. Satisfied, I grinned down at her as I held her panting and trembling body on top of me.

"Sleep, little blessing." I urged her with a kiss on her forehead. "I will tuck you into bed soon." As much as I wanted to keep her in my arms throughout the night, sleeping on a hardwood floor really wasn't good for her back.

"But you're comfy." She whined with a pout as her eyes watched my shadow hands grab her water bottle from her desk. "I hate how you take care of me so well. It's not fair." She grumbled, rolling her eyes and rubbing her face into my chest.

"I like taking care of you. It brings me a sense of joy, oddly enough." Seeing her fed, rested, and happy was all I needed to be content in life. Well, seeing and ensuring she was all of that was what made me content.

"Now, drink up, then sleep." I chuckled softly, pressing the bottle against her lips after forcing her head away from me. "Otherwise, I'll dehydrate you by making you come more tonight."

Chapter 17

Gracie

~3 months later~

"Val?"

Suddenly, my body was flipped over onto my front side. Then, no more coherent words left my mouth from my head being shoved into the bed by Valphan, who then proceeded to mount me like an animal. "Oh, shut the fuck up and take this cock like a good girl." He growled above me.

My protest dragged out into a deep moan from the feeling of my aching cunt being penetrated by his thick cock.

"That's it, that's a good little slut, always wet and ready for her demon mate to take her whenever and wherever."

Apparently, that meant in the middle of the fucking night. Damn asshole, I was actually enjoying my sleep, too, before I woke up to my bed stirring. But fuck, I couldn't complain about getting my needy cunt stuffed by his glorious cock. I had to sleep all day, and it was fine. Demon dick over sleep always.

Fisting my hair, he craned my head back, forcing me to arch my back until it ached so that he could hit my insides deeper and harder. "I'm gonna take this sweet ass after I stuff your cunt full again. I can't fucking wait any longer."

The images his words created in my mind sent shivers of excitement and fear down my spine. I've barely gotten used to having him in my pussy, and we've been fucking for months at this point. The thought of his dick in my tight ass? Yeah, not fun, initially. I mean, I've seen porn of people taking bigger in their backdoor, but that was through a lot of conditioning and practice. Me? I'd be going from zero to one-fucking-hundred.

Yeah, my ass probably won't survive tonight.

A jolt of pleasure jerked my body at the feeling of my sensitive clit being stimulated while a big dick worked all of my sweet spots. We'd barely begun, and I was already losing my mind again. It'd only been a few hours since he last screwed me stupid and tucked my sore body into bed after bathing me and making me eat and hydrate.

Actually, I was surprised at this middle-of-the-night fuck because I didn't think it was possible with how he always went back to being trapped in the closet at night. If I had my head on straight, then I'd prod at him for an answer, but that was an after-sex problem. Right now, I just needed to orgasm to my heart's content so that the pain of him taking my ass would fly over my head.

Sharp tension wrapped and snapped at my stomach with each and every single one of my orgasms, making me moan loudly from the waves of rapture that ravaged my body. "That's it, my little blessing, don't stop coming. Coat my cock good with your cum. It'll make taking your ass that much easier." His deep voice whispered hotly in my ear, making me shudder.

A sting to my backside pulled a yelping moan from my trembling body, and it didn't take long for my whimpers and sobs to fill the room with the sounds of his hands making an impact on my bubbly ass cheeks. God, I hated and loved getting spanked by Valphan during sex; something about the pain spiced things up just right. The pain heightened everything and gave the pleasure he brought upon me a nice bite that drove me up the wall just right.

"Babe, more, please, spank me until I can't sit," I begged desperately with a wiggle of my ass to urge him.

His laughter warmed the area, making me smile. "Well, when you beg like that, how can I deny you?" A harsh slap cracked the air with my pained moan, followed by another and another until every inch of my backside from the top of my cheeks down to my sit spot burned with a pleasurable ache.

My body screamed with pleasure at the feeling of his rough hands gripping my burning cheeks as he buried himself completely into me. I could feel every little throb of his cock as he emptied his load into my spasming cunt that squeezed at him to milk out every last drop he had to offer.

The feeling of him removing himself, paired with the sudden rush of his hot cum spilling out of my twitching pussy and down my thighs, made me shiver and whimper.

I was such a mess, but I didn't care. I was Valphan's little fuck-doll of a mate, and I loved it.

If only that happy thought were enough to keep the pain of my asshole being broken by his demon dick away, then that would have been great. Whatever bliss I surrounded myself in shattered like glass under heat from the searing pain of my tight asshole being forced open by his textured cock.

Yeah, it hurt like a bitch, but the twisted part of me found such joy and pleasure from the pain of it all. The line between the two blurred as I found myself letting out a silent scream from the way my stomach knotted up and snapped as my ass squeezed around Valphan's cock.

All I could do was sputter helplessly and jerk around when Valphan reached around and strummed at my clit, making me sing to his tune while he fucked my ass with no mercy.

I didn't even try to fight the onslaught of mind-breaking pleasure this new position brought on. Letting instincts take over, I felt my body react as I let my mind sink into the depths of lust. My hips slammed back against Valphan mindlessly, matching his rhythm and pace in no time, making the sharp slap of our bodies clap in the air.

And soon, the feeling of my juices joined his. Warmth cramped at my abdomen with each crash of my orgasm, causing the occasional squirt and gush of my juices when I was stimulated enough.

"Valphan, my cunt, need something in me, please," I begged after the need to be stuffed full in both holes became too much. "Something big, please."

All I could do was smile uncontrollably and moan happily at the sudden feeling of my tight walls being stretched by something solid and familiar. I don't know what he put in me, but it felt exactly like his dick. "Oh fuck, yes, Valphan, fucking ruin me, please." Every little movement exaggerated the feeling of the bumps and lines of his cock against my sensitive walls.

I was so full. I didn't think it was possible, and in reality, it probably wouldn't have been if it weren't for whatever magic Valphan worked on me. "Fuck, I love you so much."

Gripping the back of my hair, he forced my head back to consume me with a kiss as he jerked his hips harshly at me with some groans. "From the bottom of my demonic heart, I am filled with nothing but devotion for you, my little blessing." He breathed hotly against my lips.

With a deep groan, he buried himself into my ass and filled it up like he did my cunt. "Sweet Lucifer's balls. Fuck! I love you so fucking much, Gracie." He groaned against my lips before kissing me deeply.

My confusion interrupted our affectionate moment when I felt something wet hit my cheeks. I knew I had been crying, but this felt different.

Slowly, I craned my neck to the side to put an inch of space between Valphan and me. "Fawn, what's wrong? Did I do something wrong? Are you hurt somewhere?" Seeing his wet cheeks glisten under the dim moonlight twisted my gut and made my heart flip in my chest.

Pressing his lips into a thin line, he buried his face into my neck with a soft sob. "It's nothing... Just a little emotional over the fact I can't spend the whole night with you in my arms and how I'm stuck in the damn closet."

Something about his words unnerved me, mainly because I had heard them so many times over the past month. This time, though, paired with his emotions, something was definitely up.

Unfortunately, I couldn't bring myself to ruin our moment.

After Valphan held me for what felt like forever, he retreated to the closet once the pull became too much to fight. I thought our midnight fuck would be the end of tonight's surprises, but it was only the beginning.

The faint sounds of items clattering against the floor and the creaking of wood made my heart race until my eyes shot open. "Val?" A quick look over to the open closet shot down the idea swimming in my head.

Poised at the closet's entrance, Valphan glared at the room door with eyes full of hostility. His eyes remained unwavering from the door as he spoke to me. "Gracie." His grave voice chilled me rigid. "Get over here. Now!" He growled through gritted teeth while puffing his chest out menacingly. "Now!" He barked at me when I hadn't twitched a finger in his direction.

Swallowing my nerves, I scrambled out of bed to rush over to him. Only, I never did make it to him.

My feet were swept from under me, sending my body to the ground—hard. I swear, my brain rattled in my head on impact with the ground. Spots blurred my vision the moment my head hit, dazing me enough for whatever had a hold of me to drag me away from Valphan without much of a fight.

A rancid breath hit my face, causing me to gag slightly at the nauseating stench. "Shame, I was hoping you'd be ugly to make killing you easier." The room around me spun with the adrenaline surge that spurred my body into a flight-or-fight response.

Instinct took over with the adrenaline haze. I didn't even care or see who I kicked and thrashed against as long as it meant I got away and into Valphan's arms. My struggle didn't last long; an excruciating stab to my sides caused my body to freeze up with a throat-scratching scream.

"Or maybe I should keep you until you break." The voice above me cackled as I sobbed under it.

"Let her go! She has nothing to do with this!" Valphan was only a few feet from me but sounded miles away to my pounding ears.

"An eye for an eye, Gatekeeper." The raspy voice grew closer to my face, making my stomach churn with every heavy hit of his putrid breath. "You took away what was mine, so now I will take away your mate as revenge."

Valphan's aggressive voice shouted back at the being atop me. "That's not how this works! You and your wife broke the rules of nature set upon this realm by God and Lucifer, so punishment needed to follow. I didn't do what I did out of spite or other personal reasons, nor did I set out to torment you with my actions. What you are doing is not equivalent to my actions back then!" The room shook with a loud bang, like someone slamming against a door.

Everything faded over the next few seconds as the pain dulled out to nothing because of the shock. Coldness gripped and dragged my body down to unknown depths as my screams of pain faded into the background.

I thought maybe this was the end of the line for me, given how cold everything felt and how I floated in an endless darkness, until something warm drew me back from the depths of death. However, I wasn't sure how to feel when my heavy eyes finally opened, and I saw some beast-like creature crowding my space.

My mind instantly went to the events before I blacked out, causing adrenaline to surge through my veins again. Much to my surprise, the creature didn't fight back against my thrashing, unlike before. Instead of the anticipated retaliation, the creature further shocked me by slumping itself against me with a whine.

It didn't crush me under its weight or anything, though. More like it used its body to pin me so I'd cease struggling. Strangely, the slight weight paired with the warmth and firmness of its body was rather calming with how its body rumbled against me with its... Purr? Growl?

Also, it sounded crazy, but something about this wolf-like creature felt familiar. Its smell, like freshwater or snow, and its silky, soft golden brown-blonde fur reminded me so much of my other half.

Letting my body slacken underneath the beast, I slowly turned to look at the closet. Much to my horror, Valphan was nowhere to be seen, which made me go back into a panic mode.

"Valphan! Valphan!" My small body struggled to free itself from under the beast, to no avail. "Valphan! Please, where are you!?" My worst fear of finding his body lifeless deep in the closet somewhere surfaced the more time passed without an answer from him.

Then, this stupid beast on top of me got more annoying because it kept preventing me from going anywhere. Annoyance quickly turned to anger the more I glared at the beast; the thought of this beast possibly being responsible for Valphan's disappearance ground my nerves the wrong way.

So, deciding to be stupid, I directed my emotions at the beast, lashing my hands against its head and back. "Get off me, you stupid hairball! I swear, if you did anything to Valphan, I'll turn you into a rug!" Probably won't make good on that threat because I'm pretty sure the thing would gut me way before I even get a chance to reach for the knife.

"Gracie, cupcake, it's alright. I'm here."

And now I'm hallucinating. Great, just fucking great.

I didn't see Valphan anywhere, yet I clearly heard his voice. It definitely wasn't in my head either, with how clearly it projected into the area.

"Can you please stop hitting me? It's rather annoying."

Yeah, that time got me to stop real quick as the realization hit me.

With my hands slumped against the beast's back, I hesitantly move my eyes over to search for its eyes... His stormy grey eyes filled with a familiar warmth and affection.

"Fawny?"

Chapter 18

Valphan

WAKING UP TO MY mate in my arms felt like home.

Until reality shat in my face.

"I would say 'good morning,' but I'm mad at you," Gracie grumbled with her back turned to me as the two of us lazed around in her bed after waking. "All this time, I could have had a big, cuddly werewolf boyfriend to snuggle and pet and spoil..."

Is she fucking serious?

Judging by the lightheartedness of her tone, I would assume she was. On the other hand, this situation was not one to be taken lightly. I held a huge secret from her; technically, not all of it was out of the bag.

Huffing, Gracie jutted her hip at me, bumping my abdomen with her ass. "I can't believe you kept this from me like it was some life-or-death situation. I wouldn't have freaked out or anything if you had told me or showed me."

Gracie continued to mumble under her breath for a good while before turning around to face me with a soft glare. "Did you think I was going to reject you or something? Haven't I already told you and shown you how much I love you at this point? Why didn't you tell me about anything beyond using it to tease me? I mean, you could have told me what you looked like, at the very least." Damn my heart for cracking with her voice and getting burned by the sight of her tears.

Frowning deeply, I looked at her with apologetic eyes while bowing my head in shame. "I am sorry about not saying any of this before, especially after getting your hopes up by filling your mind up with fantasy after fantasy. I just..." Sighing deeply, I sunk myself further into the bed and buried my canine-like face into her stomach. "I didn't know how to bring it up to you, and honestly, I shouldn't have continued after I found out what I did about the gate."

I didn't want to look at her look of disdain when I said the last part to her; I couldn't bear any more shame right now, or I might die from it.

Unfortunately, Gracie didn't have any of it.

"Ow, ow, ow," I winced and hissed in response to her grabbing my wolfish ears and pulling at them, forcing me to pull my head back. "Careful! You should know better than to pull a dog's ears."

Shoving her tense face right up into mine, she bared her teeth at me. "You're lucky all I'm doing is pulling your ears right now." With my ears still in her palms, she twitched her hands to grab ahold of my horns to bunch both parts of me in her small hands.

Jerking my head around, she finally released me with a very violent huff and shove of my head. "You have a lot of talking to do, so I suggest you start before I make you sleep outside in the backyard tonight." She threatened with narrowed eyes.

"Excuse you? I am not a dog." I scoffed with my upper lip pulled back.

"Speak." The single word came out curt with her upturned chin.

Of course, I was confused as fuck. "What?"

"Kiss me." Gracie kept up with her stern tone, this time smiling smugly as she leaned close to me.

My body reacted to her demand before my mind could question any of it. Leaning my head in, I stuck my tongue out and licked her cheek.

"Down." She bit out right as I was about to dip my tongue into her sweet mouth.

Pouting with a whine, I relaxed my body away from her to give her some space while eagerly awaiting her next words.

As her smug lips stretched into a sarcastic smile, I couldn't help but tilt my head at her and raise a brow. "You follow my commands perfectly like a dog, and dare I say, even better than Goldie." She spoke with a stifled snicker behind her grin.

"Why, you little..." Somewhat offended, I grabbed Gracie by her sides, digging my fingers into her playfully until she laughed uncontrollably. "I don't know whether I should be offended or praise and spank you for playing me."

Grinning, Gracie reached out and held me tightly with a giggle. "You can do that after you explain yourself." She spoke into my neck while petting my head.

Relenting with a sigh, I relaxed against her body. "Besides losing control... I couldn't take on this form without losing my other because of the gate." Too late at this point, but I had no regrets.

Pulling back, Gracie grabbed my hybrid canine face and furrowed her eyes at me. "What do you mean? Like you're stuck like this forever?" She didn't sound upset or disgusted, so maybe this might go over well.

Giving her a sad smile, I carefully swept her hair out of her face. "To be free from the gate, I had to sacrifice a part of my soul... To be cursed to walk the world as nothing more than a beast for the rest of my days." Sighing heavily, I nuzzled the side of her face. "If I weren't with you, then I wouldn't care because I really don't mind living in this form. The only issue with this form is my size and beastly features that can make life a little cumbersome, but I can deal with it along with the animalistic drive."

I already towered Gracie before in my normal form, being around seven feet in height, but I was practically a mountain to her in this form at around nine feet. Normally, I posed a danger to Gracie given the stark difference between us, but like this? The danger intensified at least a hundred times. Being in this form was akin to being in a heightened state of excitement—ready to fight or hunt at a moment's notice.

"You are really starting to sound more and more like a dog, ya know?" Gracie remarked with a soft laugh and pet of my head. "Or a domesticated werewolf? I mean, you kinda look like a weird werewolf of sorts."

Snickering, she reached up and grabbed ahold of my ears, rubbing and scratching the area behind them, causing my tail to rapidly thump against the bed in response. "You are so adorable!" She squealed while rubbing her face into my chest.

Pulling back, she leaned up and kissed my snout. "It's going to take some getting used to, but we'll make it work." I couldn't help but fawn over her optimism about this whole situation and the warmth she radiated.

Sadly, the uplifting mood didn't last long as her smile slowly flipped upside down. "But... Last night, what happened exactly? I mean, I remember bits and parts, but I just remember a lot of pain and screaming." Sitting up, she looked her body up and down while patting it.

"A malevolent spirit came after me for revenge and decided to attack you to hurt me. He got his claws into you, tore you up more than I want to admit, and you blacked out from the shock." Grasping the bottom of her shirt, I pulled it up to reveal her fading scars along her left side. "After you passed out, I lost it. I couldn't bear to let anything happen to you because of me. It's also a bit of a blur for me after I shifted. When I came to, the spirit was torn to bits and sent back to Hell."

Hesitantly, I brushed my clawed fingers along her scars with a pained frown. "I shouldn't have hesitated to save you. I should have leaped out when we both sensed something was wrong." I'd never stop beating myself up for her scars and the mental trauma of last night's events. "I am sorry for being a bad mate. I swear, I'll spend forever apologizing and making up for it." I swore with sureness, peppering kisses with my tongue against her cheek.

Chuckling dryly, she patted my head and pushed me away softly. "You had a lot to give up with doing what you did. Don't apologize when I'm not even upset at you for it. I'm just thankful that you chose me over everything." I sensed no hesitation or flatness in her tone to suggest her words meant otherwise.

Grinning wolfishly, I swallowed her in a big hug. "Oh, my sweet blessing, you really are a Hell sent for me." I had expected more anger from her over the fact I hid it all from her when we agreed to keep things open between us. "But... Do you really not mind living with this form of mine?"

Scoffing playfully, Gracie rolled her eyes at me and flicked my nose. "Fawny, I love you, so nothing about you bothers me as it should." She remarked, sticking her tongue out at me. "It'll take a little time, but you're still my Valphan, werewolf demon or not."

Turning her head around, she looked at the closet with a sad smile and a distant look in her eyes for a moment. "Ya know, not gonna lie, I'm gonna miss our closet days." She mentioned with a dry chuckle before looking at me with a renewed smile. "But, we'll make new memories to make up for it." Then, her smile faltered for a second, "You really are free though? What of the gate?"

Looking past her to the closet, I smiled bitter-sweetly. "I am truly free from the closet and gate, which I destroyed after tossing the bits and pieces of the spirit through it." It didn't seem like it because everything remained in place, but the gateway was torn apart, and the runes smashed to smithereens. Everything slowly disappeared to nothing over the night because of a little thing called magic and cleaning shit up. Pretty sure I'd have my ass handed to me if Gracie woke up to her room looking like some construction site.

Humming softly, Gracie buried her face into my chest for a minute before looking up at me with reddened cheeks. "Your dick isn't bigger, is it?"

Chapter 19

Epilogue: Gracie

~5 months later~

"Are you sure you're okay with the ceremony being so casual? I kinda feel bad after seeing Stella's grand one."

Even if we had both agreed that we wanted something casual, I couldn't help but worry over the fact.

After all, this soul-binding ceremony was something huge for demons and angels, it seems like, so seeing my friend's spectacular one made me feel as if I was short-changing Valphan and his important moment in life.

Even if he assured me at least a thousand times at this point that he was more than fine with this because he didn't care much for a big celebration, I was still hesitant.

"Cupcake," Valphan sighed for the umpteenth time. "Our ceremony is literally going to start in five minutes." He deadpanned with a raised brow. "Before you get cold feet and cancel it all, really think about it. I mean, would you be happier with a huge celebration like Stella's? Which ceremony would you think back on ten years from now and smile upon as if it were the happiest moment in your life?"

Sighing defeatedly, I pouted at him because I had no good reply to his good question. Grumbling to myself, I lightly shoved Valphan's furry figure clad in nice clothing out my dressing room door. "Go wait at the altar. I'll be out there in five minutes, I swear."

Valphan was right. I wouldn't be happy one bit if I had some grand ceremony where I wouldn't even recognize more than half the people there. Granted, there were quite a few I didn't recognize from a quick look out the window just earlier, but they were people close to Valphan. To be fair, I didn't really have many on my side to invite to this ceremony. The only person here I knew was Stella and, I guess, Emma; I couldn't invite my cousins because, well, that was a can of rotten worms I didn't want to touch with a ten-foot pole.

Some other humans were out there, but they were the other entity's mates and people I didn't know.

I tried not to be too bothered by it because we planned a separate ceremony after this one, but more so for my side—a normal ceremony and celebration.

"Gracie? Girl, get your head out of the clouds. The ceremony is about to start, and you're still in your robe." Emma said with a nudge to my shoulder, gesturing at my dress still hanging in its bag.

Holding my breath, I nodded my head in response before letting the next few minutes pass by in the blink of an eye. By the time I zoned back into reality, I found myself standing at the end of the aisle in my floor-length wedding dress, decked out in strings of jewelry chains from the bottom to the illusion neckline. Honestly, I felt and sounded like a crystal chandelier—in a good way!

Every bead of jewelry scraped and jangled against each other with each step I took toward Valphan until I stood before him at the altar. "You know, I don't know why you were so insistent on me having all the crystal beads and such," I whispered, looking at my husband-to-be suspiciously.

"You'll see tonight." His toothy, wolfish grin never ceased to amuse me after all this time with him.

Yes, Valphan was still a demonic werewolf, and yes, we've made it work this whole time. We had to make a lot of adjustments to the house, mainly to accommodate his size, but we managed to get back into a nice routine again after working through Valphan's wild personality.

And, oh boy, his wild side was definitely something else. The constant ache between my legs served as a good reminder of that. I thought he was a good lover in bed before, but he was nearly insatiable in his current form. Damn demon practically had his huge cock buried in me 24/7, it felt like. On my good days, I didn't mind being fucked nearly every damn second of the day, but on ones where I had shit I needed to do or—God forbid—was on my period, yeah, those days were a pain in the ass.

Also, as much as I loved sex with Valphan, he was too much sometimes, especially with his huge cock. Thankfully, he weaved enough spells for me to make it not painful. Still, I could feel all the other effects of it every time we engaged with each other.

Remaining silent, I patiently waited for Aesophedus to finish his part while looking at Valphan with a tender smile.

My big ol' oaf looked so damn adorable in his white tunic top tucked into his black leather pants. The adorableness came from his big form being stuffed into clothes like an obsessed owner playing dress up with their dog. Valphan only ever wore a pair of loose shorts around our place, but he also went around naked more often than not.

The silence between the two of us broke upon Aesophedus, urging us to exchange our vows, a human tradition Valphan was rather insistent on having as well. Not that I minded, because this sweet moment was one I didn't want to forgo either.

"Gracie, my little blessing, my life didn't start until you came into it." The two of us paused for a second to chuckle to ourselves. "Your voice woke me to a new world, one I have the pleasure of sharing with you. Every second you taint my life is the best. I cannot wait to spend an eternity by your side, watching and helping you craft your stories for the world to indulge in."

A happy pause filled the air as Valphan smiled at me with tears in his eyes. "I will forever be grateful for every day I get to wake up to you and care for you. I will never grow tired of how your eyes light up and how your smile widens whenever I do something for you. I love how patient you are with me and my grumpy ass sometimes when I have to learn something new about this century. You never cease to amaze me with how motivated you are with your aspirations, and I will always be thankful for the effort and faith you put into me and our relationship."

Leaning down, he nuzzled his face into my cheek for a second. "I will never get over the fact that you adjusted your whole life to love me, especially when I became stuck like this. You really do love me for better or worse, and I will spend forever loving you in return. I will always treat you like the queen you are to me."

Then, he pressed his lips right against my ear. "I may be your god, the one you get on your knees for and shower with sweet kisses, but you are my goddess." Pulling back, he put his cool and calm façade back on. "And at the end of the day, I will always bow before you and worship you and the ground you walk on. I will always protect you in my arms and keep you safe from the evils of the world while you sleep."

Settling his forehead against mine, he locked his promising eyes full of adoration and devotion onto me. "I vow on my soul that I will always do right by you, remain by your side no matter what, for better or worse, rich or poor, in sickness and health, all until death." His words resonated into my soul as his gaze penetrated it.

"Valphan," I whispered with a tremble in my voice. "I never expected a demon roommate, nor did I imagine the demon lurking in my closet would someday be my soulmate. But I would never want to change a thing about how things have unfolded in my life. I'll admit to you now that I really enjoyed your little closet creeping sooner than I admitted to you before. Knowing that you are always there watching over me makes me feel safe and sound, and your shadowy touches were always so soothing to me, even if I liked to argue otherwise."

Smiling happily, I tightened my hands around his. "Sometimes I can't believe we're soulmates, but I will never take this gift from the world for granted. You are my forever as I am yours, and I can't wait to see how the rest of our life together unfolds." Brushing my thumbs over his fuzzy knuckles, I grin up at him. "The story of our life is going to be the best creation we ever write, and it will be the story that only we will ever enjoy."

Fighting back tears so my makeup wouldn't be ruined, I chewed my bottom lip for a moment before finishing my vows. "Every second with you will forever be the best time of my life, and I can't wait to spend forever with you. You are always there for me, and even though I may slack in the housework department, I swear I will make it up by spoiling you with so much affection and gratitude that your tail will fall off from all the wagging. I will always cherish you and everything we have now and will create in the time to come. I will be with you every step of eternity, for better or worse, rich or poor, in sickness and health, until death."

We firmly held each other's hands and looked at Aesophedus to continue the ceremony.

The shadow king looked between us for a second before continuing. "Once two souls are intertwined and bound, there is no going back. Do you two understand this?" Aesophedus looked at each of us sternly for confirmation before continuing. "Are you both here of your own free will? No coercion or blackmail from anyone?" And again, he waited for a positive answer from both of us before continuing.

Then, his gaze went to the small crowd, all of whom had nothing but big smiles on their faces as they eyed us with pure joy. "Is there anyone here who objects to this? Speak now or stay forever silent." His question rang through the air, and it was met with no objection of any sort.

After a slow look around the crowd, Aesophedus returned his gaze to me and Valphan. "I will ask you two again: are you absolutely certain? There is no undoing once your souls are bound." He wasn't doubting us; the question was the ceremony's formality and process.

"Yes, I am certain. I am choosing to bind my soul with Valphan's out of my own free will and sound mind even after knowing the end result." I replied to Aesophedus with a proud smile.

Without hesitation, Valphan spoke up right after me. "I have never been more certain of anything in my life, and I can't wait for forever with my little blessing." To further sweeten his words, he brought my hand up and kissed the back of it.

Much like Stella and Kastoron's ceremony, Aesophedus proceeded to procure an ancient dagger and pierced a small area of our chests.

Now, Stella did warn me that it sucked, but holy hell, it hurt like a mother fucking bitch to have my soul ripped out of my body! I nearly threw up and passed out with how much I clammed up from the pain! I mean, thankfully, I didn't because I don't know how I'd live that embarrassment down.

More fortunately, the rest of our celebration went off without a single hitch. Soon, night fell upon us, and the after-party came and went, leaving me Valphan to round back to our home as bound soulmates.

However, instead of venturing inside to our marriage bed to consummate everything, I ended up being dragged around back by Valphan. "Fawny? What?" My grunt cut my words off from Valphan, throwing me to the ground at the edge of the wooded area in the backyard.

Standing menacingly above me, he grinned down at me with the most unhinged grin full of teeth. "Sixty seconds." Reaching down, he grabbed the train of my dress and ripped it, turning my long dress to below my knees. "Run."

Wide-eyed, I scrambled to my feet, slowly backing away from Valphan with a racing heart. "W-wait? Tonight?" My breath trembled with excitement and nervousness as our conversations about having our first chase raced through my mind.

"Safe-word?" His voice gained a growl to it as he slowly advanced with heavy steps.

"Gate." I got it out in a single breath before spinning around and hightailing it away.

The adrenaline coursing through my body made me want to scream and yell out of fear and excitement about what was to come. I knew when the moment happened, then it would be intense, but I never imagined it to be this much of a rush to run from my demon lover—and we've barely started!

A roar shook and echoed through the thick, sparse wooded area, spurring my aching feet to pound against the uneven ground faster. I knew I stood no chance against him, and honestly, it was pointless for me to run, but the thrill of this blood-pumping excitement was what I wanted. No matter how much of a lazy-ass I was, the prospect of a chase through the woods to get fucked to oblivion by my demon mate gave me the perfect jolt.

"I can smell and taste your fear and excitement in the air, cupcake!"

My heart nearly froze at his growling words that sounded like they came from every direction. I didn't know which way to go! Breathing heavily, I whipped around randomly, weaving through the foliage randomly to deter him for a few seconds longer.

"You can run all you want, little blessing, but I can hear every breath from your body, every step of your feet, every beat of that racing heart of yours, and more importantly, every jingle and jangle of those beads." His voice cackled with a howl, chilling my whole body to the bone.

Cold air sliced at my airway with every inhale as I pushed my protestant body forward despite the outcome. I couldn't stop running from him now if I wanted because my instincts held the reins.

Then, everything came to a shrieking halt. "Gotcha!" Valphan's face moved from my periphery to my front side in a millisecond, causing me to slam into him.

I had screamed so loud that I was sure anyone within a ten-mile radius could hear me loud and clear, and my throat ached from the rawness at which I shrieked.

Instinctively, my hands and feet flew at him, kicking, punching, clawing, and even biting him as he forced my body back up against a large tree, where he trapped me with his massive one. "My sweet blessing, all ready for me to consume and break." His hot breath washed over my ear and neck, making me shiver and whimper as I struggled uselessly against him.

A winded grunt slammed into me from Valphan, slamming me against the tree, momentarily dazing me enough for him to restrain me with his shadow tentacles. With my wrists bound above my head and legs spread wide up in the air, I could no longer fight Valphan, and he was free to shred the rest of my clothing off until I was stark naked.

"Valphan, wait! I'm not ready to take you fully yet!" The startling sight of his painfully swollen cock, all throbbing and leaking precum, was a bucket of iced water to my face. I mean, I didn't even care or know when he stripped, but it was probably when he chased me just now.

Another of my screams—this time smaller and shorter—ripped through the air from the sudden smack to my cunt from his heavy cock after he slapped it with his huge hand. My breath hitched from the sudden jerk of my face, forcing me to look at him as he held his glistening hand accusingly in my face. "Liar. Look at how much you drenched my hand from a single slap."

Reaching down, he shoved three of his fingers into me, making me moan and thrust my hip at him. "You're fucking soaked, yet I haven't done anything but chase you through the forest like a maniac."

Putting an inch of space between us, he lowered his head down and shoved his hot tongue into my mouth, muffling every sound that came out of me and even going as far as shoving his tongue down my throat while he ran his claws up my legs. Every brush of his claws brought upon surge after surge of tingling pleasure, especially when he reached my inner thighs.

Then, a brief screech of pain jerked my body when I felt him dig his claws into my tender flesh, breaking the skin and causing my warm blood to bead out in their wake. "To sink my fangs into these luscious thighs, mhmm fuck." His words rumbled against my lips before I felt his tongue descend my body to my sensitive nipples. "And these little chocolate nipples of yours, so fucking delicious."

A sharp gasp choked my moan out as my body tensed in response to the feeling of something slipping into my ass. It wasn't his huge cock—thank God—'cause my ass wasn't completely stuffed full, and his hands were occupied with groping every inch of my body, so that only left one answer.

"Valphan, please, not so much like last time. You'll break my ass." As if that was even possible, but I had to try. Besides, the fear was always there no matter what, given the sheer difference between us.

"No." He denied me with a wicked grin. "You are going to take all I give you like a good little slut. I am going to stuff your ass just as full as your cunt when I take you as my wife tonight." His long tongue licked my cheek hungrily.

"Really claim every fucking inch of you as your husband before finally knotting you to keep you full of my cum."

Yeah, that thought really terrified me because I've never taken his knot before, something we decided to keep for our special occasion as a first for us. But I've seen it more than I could count at this point in time, and the thing was a monster on its own.

Growling lowly, he pressed my legs to open further until my thighs were almost even with the rest of my body. "Your cunt looks so good right now, just begging me to feast upon it until you can't squirt and gush anymore." Bending down, he gave me a long lick with a groan. "Too bad I need to get inside of you right now. Otherwise, I'm going to lose my fucking mind."

Then, without warning, he shoved himself balls deep into me in a single thrust, making me roll my eyes as my mouth hung open in a silent scream of pleasure. This was a typical reaction every time he penetrated me, but something about this time felt different. Everything felt heightened, and I felt more connected to him strangely. It was as if we were truly becoming one.

Delirious from the pleasure, I felt myself giving in to Valphan's actions. Every scratch along my body; slap against my clit, tits, or ass; pinch of my nipples; bite along my neck or shoulders; every thickening of the shadow dick in my ass; and every soul-shaking thrust of his cock into me brought me to a new height of rapture. There was a pain to it all, but the pain was so sweet and good—I wanted nothing but more.

"Focus on me, cupcake. I'm about to knot you for the first time, and I want you to see the effect your sweet body has on me." His deep voice brought me out of the depths of my lustful haze, and my eyes struggled to focus on his straining face as his hips picked up in pace and force.

Over a period of what felt like hours, his hips jerked out of rhythm to a halt as he let out a loud roar that shook the area. Buried fully in me, I felt the familiar throb of his cock with my tightened walls, but this time, something else followed before his cum.

Pain furrowed my face tight as I felt my stretched walls being forced to stretch more as his knot inflated. "Oh fuck! Valphan! It hurts!" I sobbed and bit through the pain of his cock, locking himself into me.

What was even more shocking was my body's reaction to it all. Yes, it hurt like a bitch, but somehow, my body decided to get off on it. Tremors of pure pleasure ravaged my body as I felt myself tighten around his knot and my hips thrust against him for some friction. "Shit... I'm coming. I'm coming from your knot."

Throwing my head back, I let out a deep and loud moan, letting myself come undone completely on his cocks in me.

"Love you... Fucking.... I love you so much, Valphan."

Warmth pressed against my cheek and all over my face. "Thank you. Thank you so much for loving me and letting me love you back."

Chapter 20

Epilogue: Valphan

~5 years later~

"Dada! Look! Clean!"

Well, now I didn't want to look to see what kind of mess my three-year-old made this time.

"Dada! Now look!"

Relenting with a sigh, I plastered a smile on my face as I turned around from the stove to look at my son, Micah.

Thankfully, I didn't have to try and keep the smile on my face because it naturally grew at the sight of Micah 'washing' a bowl with a rag.

Giving me a toothy grin, he held his toy bowl up with a triumphant smile. "Clean!" Without setting the bowl down, he clapped his hands together with a laugh.

Unable to help it, I laughed along with him proudly. I honestly expected a mess when I turned around because that was usually the case whenever he told me to look and clean—he wanted my attention to clean up his mess. So, to see him actually cleaning was so heartwarming.

Also, seeing him do that on his own amazed me because moments like these always reminded me of how life always went forward and that Micah wouldn't stay young forever.

On top of all that, it was a stern reminder that I was a damn parent. Some days I still wanted to shit myself because being a parent terrified me. I mean, taking a step back, it was simple, but when it came to applying everything I ever read in all the parenting books I could get my hands on the moment Gracie and I decided to start trying for a kid, yeah, fuck that.

The thought of fucking up as a parent somehow because I didn't say the right thing or reacted wrong really fucked me up. It wasn't so bad now after Gracie kicked some sense into my stubborn ass because she got tired of me treating our kid with gloves on. Also, she might or might not have withheld some cuddles and head scratches until I behaved...

Speaking of my lovely little mate.

Turning off the stove, I went to Micah to pick up the little munchkin. "Let's go get Mommy, yeah?" I asked in a pitched voice, poking at his sides with my fingers.

Pointing his chubby little finger down the hallway, Micah bounced in my arms. "Mommy!" He eagerly grinned and repeatedly jabbed his finger toward her office door.

Chuckling to myself, I took us over to the office, entering after knocking softly. "Little blessing, it's dinner time." I usually didn't interrupt her when she was holed up in the office because it meant she was close to a deadline or wanted to hyper-fixate in peace, but tonight was a special night.

"Mommy I hungry. Eat now please," Micah demanded with a little pout on his face, causing Gracie to chuckle and smile after turning her chair around.

Sitting there for a few seconds, she looked at the two of us with bright, wonder-filled eyes and a goofy smile. "He's so demanding like you, Fawny, I swear." She teased with a snicker as she got up.

"Stubborn like you though." I retorted with a snicker of my own before she shut me up with a kiss.

"Ewwww." Micah chimed in with a scrunched-up face, his tiny hands pushing our faces apart.

Chuckling, Gracie reached up and pinched Micah's giggling face. "Nothing 'ew' about sharing some love, little munchkin." To prove her point, she leaned up and drowned our child with kisses until he laughed up a good storm.

Then, looking up at me with grateful eyes, she hugged me tightly. "I will never get tired of being able to kiss you again." She spoke into my chest.

Returning her hug, I leaned down and kissed the top of her head. "And all it took was for our souls to merge." I mused with a chuckle.

I was no longer permanently stuck in my beastly form—thank Lucifer. Whatever parts of my old soul I had used to heal Gracie the night of her attack seeped into her own soul and silently festered within it. Then, when we had our soul-binding ceremony, that separate part rejoined the rest of me and regenerated that other missing half of my soul.

It took a good year for me to become whole again, but I was practically back to normal now. I could still shift, though, and I occasionally did because being cuddled and doted on by my little blessing was the best thing ever. Seriously, her head scratches, especially when she got the good spots behind my ear—Lucifer, those were the best.

"Fawny, I can see your tail wagging." Gracie joked, making me whip my head back to look at my behind to see if I had accidentally let some of my other features slip out of habit.

Looking back at my mate, I rolled my eyes at her and quietly slipped a hand down to pinch her bubbly ass, making her jump and squeal. "Don't poke the sleeping beast too much now, cupcake. Otherwise, you won't be able to leave the bed for days." I playfully threatened her with a smirk and kiss.

Intertwining our fingers, I led us all into the dining area and situated Micah in his highchair before serving the food. "Eat up, then go get ready for your event tonight. Stella and Kas will be over shortly to take Micah to free us until tomorrow." It was impossible not to sound a little suggestive toward the end because it was rare for us to have time to have fun.

Feigning ignorance, Gracie wandered her eyes from me to our son. "You know, last I checked, it's a full moon tonight, and I think I heard many wolves out back lately." She said nonchalantly while eating her dinner. "I heard a lot of people talking around town about some werewolves in the woods, too. The ones that make up our very own backyard."

Our tiny, wooded area had also expanded quite a bit over the years. A bad storm hit the area years back, nearly wiping out all the houses in the neighborhood. Many chose to relocate after the storm, so the city decided to let nature take over as it would. Then, as land opened up, Gracie and I shelled out some money to buy a few acres.

Gracie still gave me some grief about pawning off dead people's stuff, but many of the things brought to me as an offering back a few centuries were valuable antiques that got us a few pretty pennies.

Obviously, I saw nothing wrong about selling all that shit that cluttered up my storage. I had no use for any of that human junk, especially in this century. Besides, they were dead, so they definitely didn't need any of it; ain't no such thing as worldly possessions in the afterlife. What would they even do about it? Come back and haunt me?

Once dinner was done, I cleaned up and watched Micah while Gracie got ready for her author's event tonight. Well, I kept watch until Kas showed up with his mate to whisk Micah away for the night.

I never thought I'd send my kid away for the night with Kastoron the Prankster. Realms of home, I never thought I'd see Kastoron tie himself down with anyone, let alone have a kid of his own. I mean, I thought I was bad as an overprotective parent, but Kastoron took it to a whole new level for a longer moment than me.

With Micah out of the house, I took a few minutes to get ready myself to accompany my lovely mate to her event—play the handsome, doting husband and all. It didn't take me long to be ready since a quick shower and a few appearance spells were all I needed to look like a dashing human being out of a top-ten model magazine.

"Are you sure they're fine with watching Micah? I mean, you know how he and Killian get when they're together. I swear they are worse than Kastoron when it comes to pranks and shit." Gracie fretted as she zipped back and forth in our room, grabbing her accessories from one spot to the next.

Rolling my eyes, I stepped into her burning path, stopping her by grabbing her shoulders. "Little blessing, breathe," I swear, sometimes her anxiety was enough to give me anxiety.

Smiling soothingly, I rubbed her shoulders while I spoke. "Micah is more than fine, and you will be more than fine tonight at the event." Leaning in, I kissed her forehead longingly. "I will be right next to you every step of the way, like always."

"You have worked so hard to earn your place at this event. All those long days and nights of clawing at your brain and mine to finish book after book after book are finally paying off." Slipping my arms around her waist, I slowly pulled her to the end of the bed, where I sat down with her straddling my lap. "Not everyone becomes a best-selling author nationally, so take that win. You earned every bit of it with how much of your heart and soul you've poured into your unique stories."

"I know you don't like attention, but it'll only be a minute with a few questions. You will be perfectly fine." I assured her with a proud smile. "And even if I can't be up on the stage with you physically," pausing, I placed a hand over her heart, "I will always be with you." Quite literally, because our souls were intertwined.

Stroking her cheeks with the back of my fingers, I swept her hair out of her face. "Now, is there anything you want to get off your chest before we go?" She still seemed rather bothered after my little spiel with her—usually, a pep talk got her out of her rut.

Averting her gaze, she lightly scratched at her cheek—a nervous tick of hers. "Can we not run through the forest tonight?" That wasn't the end of it with the stagnant tension in the air.

"And?" I urged her with a concerned look.

"And no other nights? For a few months..." This pregnant pause wasn't getting any better with her words.

"Why? Are you hurt? Is something wrong?" Did she somehow fall out of love with me?

Worry after worry flooded my mind, no matter how ridiculous they were in nature.

Then, when she took my hand and smiled warmly at me, I became more confused.

"Fawny," she giggled with an apologetic smile, "Calm down. It's nothing bad, trust me." She assured me with a confident smile.

Slowly, she pressed my hand flat against her tummy. "I'm surprised you haven't found out by smelling the change in my scent or some shit like that." She joked with a soft laugh, which only increased to a full one when the look of realization crossed my face. "Better not break our bed celebrating this time about knocking me up."

Breaking out in an uncontrolled grin, I hugged her tightly and attacked her lips with passionate kisses. "Fuck, I love you so much, Gracie." I groaned against her reddened lips with a heartfelt smile.

"And don't worry about the bed this time. I demon-proofed it."

A wicked smirk crossed my little blessing's face.

"We'll see about that."

Thank you!

Scan me to leave a rating/review!

Please take a second to leave a rating/review if you enjoyed the story! Reviews and rating are so important to authors, especially indie authors like me! So, please take a second to give it some stars!

I hope you guys enjoyed this short little story and stay tuned for more to come in this standalone series! Next novella in the series will drop fall of 2024, and it'll be about triplet demons. In the meanwhile, if you want to read another shadow daddy demon, then Kastoron and Stella's story can be read in Under My Bed! I also have many more books if you want to check those out as well!

About the Author

ROSE CHASE, A DEDICATED nurse and loving mother to two boys, discovered her passion for storytelling in middle school on online forums and Wattpad. Despite her busy life, she delves into the captivating realm of contemporary romance, with a particular fascination for dark romance and morally gray characters. Through her skillful storytelling, Rose navigates the intricate dance between love, desire, and the shadows of human nature. When not saving lives or caring for her family, she immerses herself in the world of fiction, inviting readers to explore the depths of love and passion while confronting the complexities of the human heart.

tiktok.com/@rose.chase.author

instagram.com/rose.chase.author/

f

facebook.com/rose.chase.author

a

amazon.com/author/rose.chase

www.ingramcontent.com/pod-product-compliance
Lightning Source LLC
Chambersburg PA
CBHW030144010826
48973CB00002B/716

* 9 7 8 1 9 6 2 6 4 9 0 5 6 *